The Wedding Deception
Sheila Rabe

DIAMOND BOOKS, NEW YORK

If you purchased this book without a cover, you should be aware that this book is stolen property. It was reported as "unsold and destroyed" to the publisher, and neither the author nor the publisher has received any payment for this "stripped book."

This book is a Diamond original edition, and has never been previously published.

THE WEDDING DECEPTION

A Diamond Book / published by arrangement with the author

PRINTING HISTORY
Diamond edition / May 1993

All rights reserved.
Copyright © 1993 by Sheila Rabe.
This book may not be reproduced in whole or in part, by mimeograph or any other means, without permission.
For information address: The Berkley Publishing Group, 200 Madison Avenue, New York, NY 10016.

ISBN: 1-55773-897-1

Diamond Books are published by The Berkley Publishing Group, 200 Madison Avenue, New York, NY 10016.
The name "DIAMOND" and its logo are trademarks belonging to Charter Communications, Inc.

PRINTED IN THE UNITED STATES OF AMERICA

10 9 8 7 6 5 4 3 2 1

*For Candy, who still believes
in happy endings*

The Wedding Deception

A Faerie Tale

"Don't let him die!" cried little Celeste.

"You know the beast doesn't die. Don't be such a ninny," said her older sister Dorothea.

"But this part is so sad," said Celeste in a small voice.

Miss Pringle smiled at the child sitting on her lap and gave her a consoling hug. "And so," she continued, "the poor beast lay dying."

"Hurry, Beauty," urged Celeste.

"When at last the beauty returned to the castle," continued Miss Pringle, "she couldn't find the beast anywhere. She ran from room to room calling his name, but he did not answer."

"She should never have left the castle," said Emily knowingly. "If I lived in a fine castle, I should never leave it."

"But she lived with a beast," said Dorothea, the oldest and ever practical. "I should not wish to live in a castle if I had to share it with a hideous beast, no matter how fine it was."

Little Celeste tugged her governess's sleeve. "Please hurry," she said.

Miss Pringle smiled down at her. "The beauty ran out of the castle and into the garden. She found her beast there by the white rosebush, the same bush from which her father had picked that one perfect rose for his daughter." Miss Pringle's eyes misted and took on a faraway look. "The lovely girl knelt by the fallen beast, who was gasping his last breath. 'You forgot your promise,' said the beast. 'The grief I felt at having lost you made me resolve to die of hunger; but I die content since I have the pleasure of seeing you once more.'"

Little Celeste's dark eyes filled with tears and she sniffed.

"Baby," muttered Emily in disgust.

Miss Pringle merely patted Celeste's leg and continued her story. "'Dear Beast, you shall not die,' said the beauty. 'You shall live and become my husband. Here and now I offer you my hand and swear that I will marry none but you.'"

"Now the fireworks!" cried Emily triumphantly.

"Oh, yes, indeed," agreed Miss Pringle. "Suddenly the castle grounds were ablaze with all manner of fireworks. The beauty sprang up in a great alarm and looked all about."

Celeste clapped pudgy little hands. "Look down!" she cried.

Her governess smiled dotingly on her. "And what will she find when she looks down?"

"A prince!" replied Celeste excitedly.

Miss Pringle nodded. "Indeed, the beast had turned

into a handsome prince. Of course, he'd been a prince all along, but a wicked fairy had cast a spell over him, doomed him to remain a beast till some lady should come to love him for his kind heart alone."

Miss Pringle regarded her three young charges, looking first at Dorothea, the oldest at six, then the middle daughter, Emily, who was five, and little Celeste, the baby. All of them were fine-looking children. Both Dorothea and Emily had silky brown curls and dimples, and pretty brown eyes. Both were spoilt, and she knew that was as much her fault as their parents'. They would grow to be beauties, and already Miss Pringle looked at the future with a nervous eye, for she feared they would grow into selfish creatures. Three-year-old Celeste was by far the loveliest of the three, with her raven-black hair and cornflower-blue eyes. And much fuss was made over her amazing good looks whenever the children were paraded before company.

Small wonder her sisters were sometimes less than kind to her. They already saw their little sister possessed something they didn't, something that gained her extra attention, and treats from the plates of the lovely ladies who sat in their pretty sitting room or strolled in their gardens and admired the view of the Thames. Just as Cain hated Abel for his very goodness, so, too, these girls seemed to dislike their sister for something she couldn't help.

Miss Pringle thought of the story she had just told about the beauty and her jealous sisters and comforted herself with the knowledge that the Hart family was secure both in wealth and position. While they weren't nobility, they were quality. There would surely be no need for great jealousy, for each girl would be lovely and well dowered. And although there were not enough princes to go 'round these days, each of the Hart girls should surely have no trouble finding a titled, well-heeled husband.

Thank God life is not a fairy tale, thought Miss Pringle, for I should hate to see Celeste suffer the storms and heartaches that befall the people in those stories before they find their happy ending. And with that thought she forced a sudden premonition from her mind.

THE BEAUTY

1

Lord Swineburn laughed obediently, but his eyes strayed across the lawn to the fairylike creature camped at the edge of the grass, painting the scene before her. Miss Emily Hart, a pretty girl with soft brown eyes and dimples, who had been strolling happily next to him, followed his gaze and frowned. "My, but it is hot! I vow, if I do not have a cold drink this instant, I shall faint right away," she announced.

With reluctance the young man tore his gaze from the dark-haired young girl. "Then we had best take you inside immediately," he told his companion with a polite smile, turning them back inside the house.

It seemed to Emily that they were no sooner settled in the drawing room, enjoying the cool breeze that swept through the open French doors from the river, than her younger sister entered through those very doors, carrying her paper and watercolors.

Lord Swineburn jumped up. "Allow me," he offered, taking paper and paints from the girl.

She looked up at him with large, thickly lashed blue eyes, her lovely, winged eyebrows raised in surprise. "Why, thank you," she said. "If you would be so good as to set them on that table."

Lord Swineburn grinned at her and did her bidding. "Would you care to join us in a cool drink?" he offered. "'Tis terribly hot for May."

"Thank you," said the girl, pleased. "I must admit, I came in because I was thirsty."

Emily cast a sulky look at her rival, who accepted a glass from the eager young man. "I believe Mama was looking for you," she said.

The girl set down her glass. "I had best go find her directly. Excuse me."

She left the room and Emily smiled again. "Now, where were we? You were speaking of your plans for the future?"

"Er, yes," said Lord Swineburn, pulling his eyes back from the door. "We are going to start renovating the Hall as soon as the season is ended."

"How very exciting!" exclaimed Emily encouragingly. "And why all this work repairing the family house? Is it, perhaps, for"—her fan stilled and she coyly peeped over it at Lord Swineburn—"a wife?"

Lord Swineburn's face turned a light pink. He smiled and opened his mouth to speak.

"Excuse me."

It was the girl again. The young man's head turned to the drawing-room door as if it had been jerked by a string. He stood.

"Pray, do not get up," said the girl. "I don't intend to stay. It is just that I cannot find Mama, Emily. Where did you say you had seen her?"

"I am sure she must be here somewhere, dearest,"

said Emily between clenched teeth. "She was with us before we went out to walk in the garden. Why don't you go look for her again?"

The beautiful girl disappeared. "You have not yet told me who might be the lucky lady who will become mistress of your family home," said Emily silkily. Her admirer was still looking wistfully at the door. "Lord Swineburn?" she prompted, unable to keep the crossness out of her voice.

"Oh! I am sorry. I am afraid my mind wandered," he said, and Emily knew where it had wandered. Try as she would, she was unable to bring him back to the all-important subject of marriage and he soon took his watch from his waistcoat pocket and proclaimed himself a most selfish and impolite man for having stayed so long.

He had just risen to leave when Mrs. Hart rejoined them. She was still a fine-looking woman, in spite of her forty years and her harried expression. Her dark hair showed only a hint of gray and her figure was still good. "Oh, Lord Swineburn! You are leaving already?" she lamented. "I am sorry I wasn't here when you returned from your walk. There was a great calamity in the kitchen. The cream was spoilt and our chef . . . well, he is French, you see."

Lord Swineburn nodded his understanding. "I am afraid I have quite overstayed my welcome," he said.

"Not at all," said Mrs. Hart. "It was most kind of the Walpoles to spare you to us for a short visit. We look forward to seeing you in town next week at the Evershams' ball."

The young man took his leave, Miss Emily Hart smiling and waving him a playful good-bye. But as soon as he was gone from the house, her countenance changed. "Really, Mama! I wish you might keep a closer eye on Celeste. I am sure Lord Swineburn meant to propose, but she insisted on making a pest of herself, running in and out, and quite ruined everything. She is always trying to attract attention to herself."

Mrs. Hart looked distressed by such allegations. "Emily, how can you say such a thing? Why, Celeste isn't even out."

"One would never know it," said Emily crossly.

At that moment another young lady entered the room, a slightly older and prettier version of Emily. "Has Celeste stolen another of your admirers?" asked Dorothea.

"No more of mine than she has of yours," retorted Emily. She smiled cattily at her sister. "Unless you do not count the Earl of Umberland an admirer."

Dorothea blushed and her eyes narrowed. "The Earl of Umberland is not interested in a schoolroom chit," she said.

"Oh, no. He merely talks with her to be nice," said Emily. "Have you forgotten how I saw him talking with her in the hallway at our dinner party last week? And when they were done, he kissed her hand."

Dorothea pursed her lips. "Really, Mama. She is always underfoot. I was never allowed such freedom."

"Nonsense," snapped Mrs. Hart. "Your sister is certainly allowed no more freedom than you were at her age. And may I remind you that next spring she makes her come-out? A year before your come-outs both of you were allowed to attend dinner parties and other small entertainments."

"I am sure I was never allowed to do half so much

The Wedding Deception

as Celeste," insisted Emily. "'Tis just because she is the baby."

Mrs. Hart held up a silencing hand. "This is quite enough, both of you. I never saw such a pair of unnatural creatures! So worried that their little sister, who is not even out, will steal their admirers. Such nonsense! Why, Dorothea, you are as good as engaged to Umberland. And Emily, I am sure you will have brought Lord Swineburn up to scratch before the season is over. Now, I'll hear no more complaints about your sister."

"Yes, Mama," said each girl meekly.

Mrs. Hart smiled, in charity with her daughters once more. "Now, my dears. As we have the Finches coming to dine tonight, I suggest you both retire to your rooms and take a nap as I intend to do." With that she left her daughters to do as they wished and headed for the peace and quiet of her boudoir.

Emily flopped onto the sofa, a pout carved on her pretty face. "Sometimes I hate Celeste," she announced.

"Be glad you are a year older. At least you were able to make your come-out before her," said Dorothea. "You should have Swineburne safely engaged to you before the month is out."

"And do you intend to have Umberland?" asked Emily curiously.

"Of course," said Dorothea with a haughty toss of her head. "An earl is a fine enough prize. I'd be foolish to hold out another season."

Emily nodded her understanding. There was no need to say that next season Celeste would be on the Marriage Mart, making the competition stiff, indeed.

Meanwhile the subject of their discussion had finally found her mother. "Did you need me, Mama?"

she said, peering around her mother's bedroom door.

"No," said Mrs. Hart. "Whatever made you think that, dearest?"

"Emily said earlier you were looking for me."

Mrs. Hart nodded with sudden understanding. "Come to think of it, I was looking for you earlier, my poppet. But I cannot for the life of me remember now why I wanted you." She smiled at her daughter and beckoned her into the room.

Celeste entered and knelt in front of her mother's chair.

The woman took the girl's chin in her hand and smiled dotingly on her. "Perhaps I simply wished for the pleasure of seeing your sweet face," she said.

"Oh, Mama," said Celeste, blushing. "You know I am not half so pretty as Dorothea and Emily."

"So they tell you," said her mother.

"But it is true," insisted Celeste. "I wish I were as beautiful as you."

"You are ever so much more beautiful than I, my poppet. And, most important, you have an unselfish heart, which is the beauty most treasured by a wise man. Remember that." She smiled again and gave her daughter's chin a playful squeeze. "Now run along, child, and let me get my rest. We have company coming to dinner tonight."

Company for dinner! The prospect was terribly exciting. Celeste always felt rather low when her sisters went off to a ball or rout or al fresco breakfast and she was left behind at home. But company, that was a different story. She was allowed to try her social wings a little when company came. And it was always such fun. Some of the young ladies looked at her queerly, but the gentlemen were invariably kind, many promising to dance with her when she had her come-out ball next spring.

As she made her way downstairs that evening, in a jonquil gown with puffed sleeves and a modest neckline, she thought with anticipation about the fine dinner they would have, and wondered whether that handsome Edward Finch would speak to her. Mr. and Mrs. Finch had both a son and a daughter. The daughter was Emily's age and not so very friendly. But her brother, who was a year older, was very nice. He had spoken with her at great length when they'd gone to the Finches' to dine and had even offered to show her some rare plants in the conservatory—until Emily had come along and swooped down on him like a giant bird taking him away. It had been very wicked of Em, really, for Edward had been speaking with her. And besides, Emily already had an admirer—that nice Mr. Swineburn.

"Celeste," said a sharp voice behind her. She turned to see her sister Emily. "I hope you don't intend to make a cake of yourself over Edward Finch tonight," Emily cautioned as they made their way downstairs. "It reflects poorly on the rest of us."

"I never made a cake of myself over Mr. Finch," said Celeste, stung. "All I did was talk to him. And he started it."

"That is what you always say," said Emily crossly.

"But 'tis true!" protested Celeste.

"Just remember, if you are too forward and talk too much before you have even been presented at court and had your come-out ball, people will think you are fast," cautioned Emily, and swept on ahead of her.

Celeste stuck out her tongue at her sister's back.

Lemon face, she thought. You have become as insufferable as Dorothea.

When they were small, Emily had been much more fun. And kinder, often taking her side when Dorothea bullied her. But the last two years had changed Emily. Now it seemed that, just like her older sister, she spent all her time preening before her looking glass. Or helping Dorothea to bully their little sister—always telling her not to talk so much, shooing her away whenever callers came. Really! It was most insulting.

Well, I shall be out next year, Celeste consoled herself. Then you shan't be able to order me about as if I were a child.

With that pleasant thought she made her way to the drawing room, where the newly arrived guests stood visiting with her family.

Her father caught sight of her as she entered the room and beamed. "Here's my little beauty now," he said, holding out an arm to her. "Don't you look lovely tonight?"

Celeste blushed and smiled. "Oh, Papa."

Edward Finch, who had been standing with the men, seemed to agree, for he was looking at her in a way that made her feel like a sweet on display in Gunther's and deepened the pink flush on her face.

"Nice to see you again, Miss Hart," he said politely.

"And it is nice to see you again, Mr. Finch," she replied. "I was so sorry you were never able to show me those lovely plants in your conservatory when we were last with you. I wish I had some such treat to offer you here, but alas, I don't. Unless you should like to see Papa's hothouse orchids. But then, I am sure you have orchids in your own hothouse."

Mr. Hart's bushy eyebrows rose and Mr. Finch

looked questioningly at his son, who blushed and coughed but was spared giving any explanations about his suspicious offer by the arrival of the butler to announce dinner.

The meal was a lively affair. Both the elder Hart sisters were in fine form, witty and charming, and Miss Finch, also. She paid little attention to Celeste, on her right, but had much to say to Emily. Of course, reasoned Celeste. They had both been presented together. They attended the same balls, knew the same people. It was natural she should prefer to talk with Em. Celeste sighed and took a mouthful of peas. Almost, she wished she had taken her dinner upstairs with Miss Pringle.

After the meal the ladies left the men to their port and retired to the drawing room. While the two mothers visited at one end of the room, the young ladies sat in another corner and compared notes on the various men they'd met.

"I think the Earl of Warwicke is terribly handsome," confessed Miss Finch.

"Did he not ask you to dance at the Hemphills' ball last week?" asked Dorothea.

Miss Finch nodded and sighed. "But he also asked Lady Mary Mortley, too. Twice."

"I believe his family expects him to marry a title as well as money," said Dorothea.

"But the viscount has been showing a marked preference," said Emily encouragingly. "I hear he has fifty thousand pounds a year."

Miss Finch shrugged. "He will do."

"You don't sound as if you like him very well," observed Celeste.

Miss Finch looked at her in surprise. "What has that to do with it?"

"But you do not love him?" persisted Celeste.

Dorothea shook her head. "She is still fond of fairy stories, our sister," she explained.

Miss Finch gave Celeste a condescending look and the three young ladies continued their calculating assessment of the various eligible gentlemen of the ton.

The papas and Edward joined the ladies and the conversation once more took a lively turn, Dorothea and Emily both being careful to monopolize young Edward's attention so he couldn't flirt with Celeste.

She didn't mind. She was busy mulling over all she had just heard. How very cold-blooded this husband hunting seemed! Would she change in another year and become like Dorothea and Emily, a cold, calculating female, inspecting a man much as if he were a bolt of cloth at Grafton House? She certainly hoped not. She wanted to be happy and in love, like her mama and papa. Surely not everyone thought as her sisters and Miss Finch.

"Give us a song, Emily, love," her papa was saying.

"If you wish, Papa," said Emily, the perfect picture of the obedient daughter. She glided gracefully to the pianoforte and settled herself, favoring the company with a song. Not to be outdone, Mr. Finch suggested his daughter join her in a duet.

The two young ladies made a pretty picture, Emily seated at the pianoforte, Miss Finch standing behind her, a delicate little hand resting on Emily's shoulder.

Edward Finch took advantage of his sister's absence to take her chair next to Celeste's. "A very pretty picture," he whispered, and Celeste agreed, thinking he was referring to his sister and Emily. If anyone had suggested he was referring to her as she sat listening, she would have been amazed.

The girls ended their concert and returned to their seats, Emily making sure she gained a seat next to Edward, as well as his attention.

Dorothea was called upon to entertain the guests with her harp, and by the time she was done the supper tray was being wheeled in. The Finches took their tea and cakes and cheeses, then took their leave. The older Hart sisters stood on either side of Mr. Edward Finch, lavishing attention on him to the last. Both sisters looked anything but pleased when he craned back his head in search of Celeste, standing beside her papa, and bid her a fond farewell.

2

"THERE! I HOPE you are happy with yourself," said Dorothea. "Throwing yourself at Edward Finch in such a fast way."

Celeste's mouth dropped. "Throwing myself at him?" she repeated. "I have no idea what you are talking about."

"Oh, such innocence," scoffed Emily. "Just as you had no idea you might be interrupting something today when Lord Swineburn came to call."

"Why, no," said Celeste. "Why should I have? He invited me to join you."

"What else could he do? You were there."

Mr. Hart frowned at the turn his enjoyable evening had taken. When they were little, he had doted on all three of his lovely daughters, dandling them on his knees, bringing them home special treats whenever he went to London on business. But as the years went by and the little girls grew to womanhood, he began to notice that all was not always sweetness in his house.

And that was certainly true this night. Feminine voices were rising dangerously. "Enough!" he commanded. "I'll not have my daughters quarreling like a shopkeeper's girls. Now off to bed, all of you, and let us hear no more of no such nonsense."

"But, Papa," began Emily.

"I've had quite enough, puss," he said sternly.

Emily tossed her curls and followed her tight-lipped older sister up the stairs.

Celeste, who had shrunk back against her father during her sisters' accusations, looked up at him with teary eyes. "Papa, I never tried to steal Lord Swineburn from Emily. Really, I didn't."

"I know, child," said Mr. Hart wearily. He smiled at her and gave her shoulder a pat. "Off with you now." She stood on tiptoe and kissed his cheek and ran off up the stairs after her sisters.

Mr. and Mrs. Hart followed at a more sedate pace, he shaking his head. "Feminine hysterics," he muttered irritably.

"Have you noticed a change in Dorothea and Emily over the years?" he asked his wife later that night.

She smiled. "I've noticed many. I believe it is called growing up."

Mr. Hart shook his head. "I don't mean physical changes. It is something else. Sometimes the girls seem rather—" He stopped, at a loss for words.

"Spoilt?" supplied his wife. "They are indeed, I am afraid. We have indulged them sadly."

Mr. Hart sighed. "I cannot say I liked the way they behaved after our guests left tonight."

"Nor can I," agreed his wife. "But I am afraid it is too late to change them now."

* * *

By the following morning hostilities had been dropped in the excitement of returning to London. Though Mr. Hart disliked the city in the heat and preferred to run away occasionally to his modest riverside seat in Middlesex, his daughters didn't share his views. Instead of thinking it a treat to escape the unseasonal spring heat, they considered themselves deprived for having had to miss six days of the season and were excited to be returning to town. As their carriage made its way toward London all three girls chattered happily.

Their father smiled fondly at his daughters, obviously happy to see them getting along once more. Dorothea, who missed nothing, took advantage of his charitable mood by extracting a promise of a new ball gown from him.

And she made sure they set out the day after their return to choose the material for it.

She wanted to visit a very exclusive and high-priced shop in Leicester Square, but her mother firmly said they would visit Grafton House, "for I know your father has been concerned of late about how much we are spending this season, and I'll not squander money needlessly."

Dorothea looked less than pleased by this speech, but said nothing.

Celeste followed her mother and sisters into the large establishment, her eyes wide with delight. Shopping! It was all so exciting, she thought, watching the beautifully dressed ladies browsing among the ells of silk, satin, and velvet. So many colors and textures. However would Dorothea choose?

"Oh, Mama," breathed Dorothea, fingering a delicate blue silk. "This is lovely."

"That color will look very nice on you, dear," said Mrs. Hart.

"Mama!" Emily caught her mother's arm. "There is the prettiest pink-and-white-striped muslin over on that table. It would make a perfectly charming morning gown."

"Now, Emily. You know we came to purchase material for a ball gown for your sister."

"Yes, but this is not so very much," wheedled Emily. "And you know I have been needing a new morning gown this age." Her mother hesitated and Emily continued to plead.

Mrs. Hart finally gave in and was rewarded by a hug from her daughter. She turned, smiling, to her youngest. "And you, my poppet? What would you like?"

"I would like Papa to take me to Madame Tussaud's to see the wax figures," said Celeste.

Her mother laughed. "That is certainly less costly than our expedition today. I am sure such a price your papa will gladly pay. And next year you will get your ball gown."

Celeste smiled, content to wait for the golden future.

The dressmaker was unable to finish Dorothea's new ball gown in time for the Evershams' ball, but she looked lovely nonetheless, the pale green of her satin gown showing off her creamy skin and brown hair. "You look wonderful," said Celeste as the footman draped capes over her sister's shoulders.

"Thank you," said Dorothea.

"You too, Em," added Celeste.

Emily checked her reflection in the front-hall mirror one last time and smiled at what she saw. "It will do," she said.

"And what shall you and Miss Pringle do tonight, my poppet?" asked her mama.

"Oh, we shall play at piquet, I imagine. Poor Miss Pringle. I am afraid the only time she beats me is when I cheat in her favor."

Her father chuckled. "You are wasted here. I should take you with us tonight and bear you off to the card room with me."

"Papa. We should be going," urged Dorothea.

"Then let us be out the door," said Mr. Hart, smiling, and Celeste noticed it was rather a weak smile, as if he were very tired.

"Papa, are you feeling quite well?" she asked.

"Certainly. Never felt better," said her father heartily. "Come, my girls. Let us be off."

They were gone in a swirl of capes and silks. Celeste listened to the clack of the horses hooves as they pulled the carriage away to the ball and bit her lip. Papa had certainly looked tired to her.

Her family did not return till long after Celeste had gone to bed, so she did not hear until the following morning of Dorothea's triumph. The Earl of Umberland, it seemed, was about to be brought up to scratch. He had asked to wait upon Mr. Hart that very morning. Dorothea was in ecstasies.

"Oh, milady. Will you allow me to call on you at your country seat?" begged a teasing Emily.

"Of course," replied Dorothea graciously. "My doors will always be open to all my relatives." She turned to Celeste. "Once I am married, I shall be a great help to you," she said. "I shall be able to find you a rich and titled husband from among Umberland's acquaintance."

Celeste preferred to find her own husband, but was touched by her sister's kindness. "Thank you," she said. "I'm sure you will be very happy with the earl."

Dorothea smiled. "I shall enjoy being a countess," she predicted.

Before the earl called, another man paid a visit to Mr. Hart. The two men were closeted for some time in the library.

Celeste had seen her father's visitor and noticed he didn't look particularly happy. Bad news? She lingered outside the door, anxious to know why the man had come, hoping the strong presentiment pressing hard on her spirit was simply imagination.

Before even half an hour had passed, the library door opened and the two men came out. Celeste looked at her father's white face and knew something terrible had befallen him. "Papa!" she cried, and ran to him.

"There now, my girl. What's this?" said Mr. Hart, trying to look cheerful.

"Something is wrong, isn't it?"

"Nothing is so wrong it cannot be fixed," said Mr. Hart cheeringly. He turned again to the man, thanked him for his kindness, and bid him good-bye.

The man took his hat and gloves from the butler and left, looking relieved to make his escape.

Celeste still clung to her father. "What has happened?" she cried.

"Nothing that need concern you, my child. Now go along and paint me a pretty picture. I have much to

The Wedding Deception

do." He shooed her off and turned back into the library.

Celeste stayed in the hall, wringing her hands, wondering what could be wrong. She watched a footman enter the library and knew her father had rung for him, probably to ask him to summon her mother. The footman left and soon she saw her mother approaching. "Oh, Mama! What is wrong?"

Her mother looked surprised. "Why, what on earth can you mean, child?"

"Something is very wrong," said Celeste. "A man came. He went into the library with Papa. He did not look happy. And when he came out, Papa looked terrible, like he'd seen a ghost."

Fear spread across Mrs. Hart's face as her daughter spoke and she rushed past her into the room.

Celeste took a step to follow her then thought better of it. Instead she hovered near the door. Finally, unable to bear the tension any longer, she put her ear to the heavy door in the hope of hearing something. All she could hear was the muffled sound of voices. She pressed her ear harder to the thick oak. Only a few moments passed before she heard her mother make a sound like a wounded bird and heard her father cry out. "Elizabeth!"

Celeste threw open the door and saw her mother on the library sofa in a faint, her father bending over her. He looked up. His face was whiter than it had been when last she saw it and now he looked angry. "Celeste! I told you to leave. Do not make me repeat myself."

"But Mama," began Celeste.

"Leave!" commanded her father.

Celeste fled to her room.

Later that morning the Earl of Umberland called on Mr. Hart. The two men were closeted in the library for some time.

Dorothea, upstairs, waiting for a summons to the drawing room where the earl would bow upon one knee and offer her his heart and all his worldly goods, was pacing. "What can be taking them so long?" she demanded.

Emily sat on her sister's four-poster bed, keeping her company. "I suppose there are a great many details to be worked out when a marriage is planned. Dowries and such."

Dorothea checked her appearance in her looking glass and took another nervous turn about the room. "Should I let him kiss me?" she asked.

"You will be engaged," said Emily. "I suppose you should."

Dorothea smiled and did a little pirouette. "Within the year I shall be a countess."

Emily hugged her knees. "And I shall be a viscountess," she said dreamily.

Dorothea cocked her head. "You think Swineburn will propose?"

"I've no doubt of it."

The two girls smiled.

Outside came the sound of departing horses. Dorothea ran to the window and looked out. "Umberland's leaving!" she cried.

Emily joined her and peered out the window just in time to catch of glimpse of the earl's curricle before it rounded the corner.

The sisters looked at each other, mystified.

There was a knock on Dorothea's door. She opened it and saw Jarvis, the footman. "Your father would like to have a word with you, Miss Dorothea. And Miss Emily, too. In the morning room."

Again, the two girls exchanged looks, worry edging onto their faces. They hurried downstairs to find their father and mother seated together on the sofa, both looking pale and drawn. Celeste arrived shortly after them and all three girls seated themselves and looked expectantly at their father.

"I am afraid I have some hard news for you, my girls," said Mr. Hart. "I want you to try to take it bravely, like the sweet girls I know you are."

There was panic on Dorothea's face now. "Papa, what has happened? Why did the earl leave without proposing?"

"I am afraid he is not going to be able to marry you after all, my dear," said Mr. Hart.

Dorothea jumped up. "What! What can you mean? Is that not why he called on you?"

Mr. Hart nodded. "Yes, that is why. But I'm afraid we have had some bad news this morning. I have made some poor investments on the 'change."

"What does that mean?" asked Emily.

"It means I have gambled with our future and lost," said her father flatly. "I am ruined."

"Ruined?" echoed Emily.

Dorothea sat staring woodenly. Her father came to her and took her hand. "Our financial position has changed, nearly overnight, I'm afraid. The earl must marry a woman of fortune. His family expects it of him. He cares deeply for you, my dear, but his position demands . . ."

Dorothea slumped in her chair, eyes closed.

Mrs. Hart had been prepared. She knelt by her daughter and held a little vial under her nose. Dorothea's head jerked away and her eyes fluttered open. She moaned and stared at her father as if still trying to comprehend his words.

"What does this all mean?" demanded Emily.

"It simply means, my dear, that our London season is at an end. We must let the town house to someone else for the remainder of the season."

"John, will that be possible?" asked his worried wife.

Mr. Hart shrugged. "We must try." He turned again to his daughters. "We will, most likely, have to sell our home and find something smaller, less costly." Here the poor man's voice broke.

"Oh, Papa." Celeste took her father's arm. "I am so sorry."

He looked sadly down at her. "No. It is I who must be sorry, child, for I have ruined your prospects. I do not know what will now become of us."

"Papa, how could you have done such a thing?" wailed Dorothea.

"Dorothea," he began.

Tears were coursing down his oldest daughter's cheeks. "Oh, don't speak to me. I vow I shall never speak to you again as long as I live. I shall be an ape-leader now and it is all your fault." She turned and ran from the room, her loud sobs echoing back to them.

"Lord Swineburn will still have me," said Emily in a small voice. She turned pleading eyes to her mother. "Won't he, Mama?"

Mrs. Hart looked at her daughter with worried eyes. "Let us hope he will, dear."

Emily blinked several times, trying to hold back the

tears. Finally she failed. The sobs broke from her and she, too, fled the room.

Mr. Hart turned to his youngest daughter. "Do you, too, hate me, child? I have ruined your future as well."

Celeste hugged him. "No, Papa. You've not ruined my future at all. I never wished to marry, except for love. And if I find no one to love me, then I shall be content to stay with you and Mama, even if we must share a small cottage."

With that her father himself was overcome with sobs and ran from the room, leaving Celeste and her mother staring after him.

Word spread quickly of the Hart family's ill fortune. Many friends wrote or called with condolences. But none came with offers of marriage. The family left London, and the gay social whirl of the ton became nothing but a painful memory. In fact, many of the luxuries the family once enjoyed fast turned to memories. Most of the servants were let go and new gowns became something only to be dreamed of.

Dorothea refused to be comforted. True to her word, she had not spoken to her father, who looked more pale and wan with each passing day. Her mother upbraided her for her coldhearted behavior, but the girl would not unbend. "He has ruined my life," she said. "Why should I wish to speak to someone who has ruined my life?"

"Shame on you," scolded Mrs. Hart. "What a wicked girl you have grown into! Your father has doted on you since the day you were born. Everything he did he did for you."

"Did he lose his fortune for me?" countered Dorothea. "Did he think I should be happy as an old maid? How very thoughtful of him."

Mrs. Hart's lips compressed into a thin, angry line and she boxed her insolent daughter's ears. "Heartless, unnatural child! Do you think he meant such a thing to happen?"

Even in the face of her mother's wrath Dorothea remained unrepentant, continuing to blame her father for her misfortune and refusing to speak to him.

Celeste wandered the house like a ghost, trying to memorize every dear corner of it, for she knew their days there were numbered. How she would miss it, she thought.

Edward Finch called and offered for Emily, who was delighted to take him, as Lord Swineburn had ceased to call when the family's misfortune became public knowledge. And, as Edward Finch was a fine-looking young man from a wealthy family, she felt herself well pleased with the deal. She danced merrily around the house, humming, while her older sister scowled.

"It isn't fair," Dorothea complained one day to her mother. "I am the eldest. Edward should have offered for me."

"Perhaps that horrid look you've worn on your face these past two weeks scared him," suggested Mrs. Hart.

"Such ill fortune would make anyone miserable," said Dorothea in her own defense.

"Everyone suffers ill fortune at some time or other in their lives," said Mrs. Hart. "The ones who allow it to change them for the worse are the ones who suffer most."

Dorothea said nothing to this, but her mother noticed a thoughtful look on her daughter's face and took hope.

And she took hope when a letter from Gloucestershire arrived for her husband and he burst excitedly from the library, calling her name. She turned to Celeste and said, "My poppet, I believe our fortunes are about to change."

3

THE LETTER MR. Hart had received was from none other than the Duke of St. Feylands, a distant relation of the Harts. News of their sad circumstances had reached him at his castle in the Cotswolds.

"The offer he has sent us is so generous as to be nearly beyond belief," Mr. Hart told his family, whom he had called into the morning parlor.

"He is sending us money?" guessed Dorothea.

"No. Better than that," said Mr. Hart.

Dorothea said she couldn't imagine anything more generous than the offer of enough money to end their troubles.

"This will do the same," Mr. Hart assured her. "The duke has offered to take one of you to stay as his guest at St. Feylands. You shall remain for a period of at least three months, and if you prove satisfactory in both mind and deportment, you shall become the Duchess of St. Feylands."

All three girls sat gaping at their father in amazement.

"Why, I cannot credit it," gasped Mrs. Hart. "The duke must be sixty if he's a day. I should never have imagined him in the market for a wife."

"Perhaps he was not before he heard of our misfortune," said her husband. "This is his way of helping us."

"A duchess," said Emily with awe. "How I wish I had not accepted Mr. Finch."

"Be glad you have," said Dorothea. "Would you really want to marry the beast, even if he is a duke?"

"Dorothea!" scolded her mama.

"It is what we used to call him when we were small," said Dorothea defensively. "Because he lived in a great castle and was so very mean and ferocious, just like the beast in Miss Pringle's fairy tales." She turned to her sisters. "Remember how he got after us for playing hide-and-seek in his bedroom?"

Emily nodded. "It frightens me even now to remember it," she said. She turned to her father. "Who is to go?" she asked.

Mr. Hart rubbed his chin thoughtfully. "Well, I suppose you are out of the running, Emily, as you are already engaged."

Emily heaved a sigh of relief.

Mr. Hart's gaze fell on his oldest daughter, who shrank back against her chair. "Oh, not me, Papa. Please. I still want to marry the earl. If he hears someone as rich as the Duke of St. Feylands has befriended us, I am sure he will offer for me."

"But Dorothea, you must be the one," said Emily. "*Someone* must marry the duke to save the family. *I* cannot, for I am already engaged, and Celeste is not yet even out."

"But I am almost out," said Celeste. "In another year I should have been. If I were to stay with the duke for six months and marry in another six, I should be plenty old enough to be a bride."

"To a man old enough to be her grandfather," said Mrs. Hart miserably. "John, we must refuse. I'll not see Celeste sacrificed like this."

"But, Mama," protested Dorothea. "She must go. She is the only one without a prospective husband. What will become of us if she does not?"

"You mean what will become of you?" said Celeste in a low voice.

Dorothea stared at her, shocked by a remark so out of character.

Celeste returned her sister's look with one of ice. "I do not offer to do this to help you," she said. "For you have been so cruel to Papa you deserve a terrible fate." She smiled at her parents. "I wish to do it for Mama and Papa. I shall go."

"Absolutely out of the question," said Mr. Hart firmly.

"You must let me," said Celeste. "Besides, it will be a great adventure," she added brightly.

"John." Mrs. Hart's voice was pleading.

"Papa, she wants to go," said Dorothea. "She wants to be a duchess."

"Do you really wish to do this, my child?" asked Mr. Hart. "If you do not, you have but to say the word. We shall manage."

How? thought Celeste. Surely living with a cranky old duke could be no worse than living with an angry Dorothea, watching her turn into a bitter old maid.

Dorothea was right. Their family needed the duke and his wealth. And Celeste was the only one who could go. If she did not, Papa would have to sell their beautiful home on the Thames. And it would quite break his heart. What would become of them? Where would they live? Surely the fates had handed them deliverance on a silver platter. She must take it, for all their sakes.

She thought her face would crack from the effort, but she put on a smile. "Yes, Papa. I truly wish to do this. You must write the duke straightaway, before he changes his mind."

"Very well," said Mr. Hart sadly.

"Oh, John. How *could* you?" demanded his wife after the girls had left them.

"What choice did I have?" he asked.

"How did St. Feylands learn of our distress?"

"I wrote him."

Mrs. Hart looked at her husband as if he had just confessed to a murder.

"Do not look at me so, Elizabeth. I certainly did not write to the ogre to offer up a virgin daughter. I had hoped he might loan me a little something to help me get on me feet. After all, we have a connection, although it is not one I would be quick to claim under any other circumstances. This offer was most unexpected.

"And, I must admit, when first I read his letter I was quite overjoyed, for I had thought to send Dorothea. She has always fancied a title and I felt sure she would be thrilled. I never dreamed—" His voice broke.

"My poppet, my baby," mourned Mrs. Hart. "Oh, however can I bear it?" She pressed her face in her hands and cried.

Her husband took her in his arms and tried his best to comfort her. "Now, dearest. Don't cry so. 'Tis not as if we'll never see her again."

"It will be close enough," sobbed his wife. "And to marry her to such an old, cranky man!"

"Who will most likely be a doting husband."

"Who will bellow and throw his slippers at her, most like," said his wife. "Don't forget I've met the man. An ill-tempered fellow he was when we visited him ten years ago."

"He had lost his young wife only two years before," said Mr. Hart.

"And whatever kindness he once possessed," added Mrs. Hart.

Both husband and wife fell silent, each lost in their own thoughts. Mrs. Hart began to cry again and her husband held her silently, unable to find any words of comfort for either of them.

Upstairs, Celeste was trying to find some thought with which to console herself. She didn't remember the duke well, but she did have a fuzzy memory of a great, gray-haired, roaring man, and of herself trying to shrink behind dusty velvet curtains so he wouldn't find her. Oh, dear, she thought. But she had been a child then, a naughty child. Surely now that she was a grown woman the duke would not treat her so. And perhaps Mama would allow her to take Smythe with her. She smiled at the thought of how taking the family's one remaining abigail would discomfort Dorothea. Yes, she would definitely take Smythe. It would be comforting to have a familiar face with her in her new surroundings.

The proposed loss of Smythe, did, indeed, make Dorothea unhappy, but considering her sister's great sacrifice, she deemed it wise not to make too great a fuss.

The day of Celeste's departure finally arrived. She and the abigail climbed into the Duke of St. Feylands's crested carriage, which had been sent to fetch them, and after watching till both family and home were out of sight, clung to each other as they were whisked off to their new life at the castle of the "beast."

THE BEAST

4

St. Feylands was a castle even more grand than Celeste had remembered. "Oh, my," she said in awed tones as the carriage drove past the gatehouse with its two rounded towers and into the park. She peered out the window. At the end of the long drive sat the castle itself, an impressive stone edifice dating back to the twelfth century.

As the duke's carriage drove up to it she wondered how she'd ever be able to find her way around in such a huge and rambling structure.

They were met by a solemn-looking groom of the chambers, who welcomed Celeste to St. Feylands and informed her he would be happy to show her to her room. As he spoke two servants went out to the carriage to bring in her trunks.

Imagine! thought Celeste, a servant just to show one about and more to carry one's trunks. Even when Papa's fortunes were good, they never had such an abundance of servants. The Duke of St. Feylands must be very rich, indeed.

Celeste followed the man up a wide, curving staircase, her abigail following behind. Mrs. Griffon, the housekeeper, he told her, would be happy to acquaint her with the castle the following morning. This was good news, she thought as they made their way down a shadowy hallway, for she was already feeling lost.

"The duke does not keep town hours," continued the man. "Dinner is served at half past six."

The duke! Celeste wondered if he was still as ferocious as he had seemed to her when she was a child. She supposed she would have to wait till dinner to find out, for it would appear her host did not mean to show himself until then.

Her bedchamber proved most satisfactory. Fresh flowers sat on the table by a curtained French sofa bed. In one corner of the room was an escritoire, in another a couch of gilt beechwood, upholstered in a cream-colored material with pink stripes. Against one wall was a cupboard large enough to accommodate the gowns of both her sisters, and placed to catch the light from the window was a dressing table with an elaborately framed looking glass. "What a pretty room!" she exclaimed. She turned to her abigail. "It would appear the duke wishes me to be happy here."

"Indeed, it does," agreed Smythe, taking her mistress's cloak. "I suppose the flowers were the housekeeper's idea," she ventured.

"Oh, yes." Celeste had preferred to think the flowers her host's idea. But, of course, putting flowers in a room was something a man wouldn't think of. She went to her bedroom window and looked out. The castle grounds seemed to go on forever, lush and verdant, and inviting.

Smythe already had her trunk open and was hanging dresses in the cupboard. "Would you like to rest, miss?" she suggested.

Actually Celeste was dying to explore the castle and the grounds, but no one had suggested such an outing to her this afternoon, and she felt timid about setting off on such a bold venture on her own. It was now only three o'clock and the dinner hour of six-thirty seemed a long way down the corridor of time. She sighed. "Yes, I suppose I would." Though how she could relax when her interview with the beast still lay ahead of her she could not imagine.

Although sleep had seemed impossible, once Celeste was snug under the coverlet, she found that the excitement and arduousness of her journey had left her body tired, and before she knew it, her energetic mind had been lulled into a state of slumber.

At four-thirty, however, she awakened and found herself unable to get back to sleep. Smythe had lain down on the little trundle bed in the dressing room and Celeste felt loath to wake her. What to do until dinner? Perhaps just a peek around the castle?

She got back into her gown as best she could and threw a shawl around her shoulders. She opened her door and peered out. A long hallway lay in either direction, shut doors on both sides. Perhaps the lower part of the house wouldn't seem so forbidding.

Feeling very much like a child escaped from the nursery, Celeste tiptoed down the large, curving staircase. The entryway loomed before her, large and empty, yawning like some evil genie's cave. She caught the sound of footsteps approaching from another section of the castle and fled back up to her bedroom.

Once inside, she heaved a sigh of relief. Well, perhaps it would be best to wait till the morrow and let Mrs. Griffon conduct her on a tour of the house.

Looking at the escritoire, she decided to begin a letter home. *Dear Mama*, she wrote. *I am safely arrived at the castle St. Feylands. It is a most impressive structure.* Terrifying was more the word, but she could hardly upset her mother with such a description. She dipped her quill and resumed her writing.

My room is very pretty. It contains a comfortable bed, on which I have already rested, a lovely escritoire, at which I presently write, and the prettiest little sofa on which to recline and read novels. The duke has had fresh flowers placed on the table near my bed, which was most thoughtful of him. She paused and bit her lip. The duke. What to say about him? She had thought it very odd he had been nowhere in sight when she arrived and that he'd made no effort to welcome her to his castle, but again, this was hardly something she could put in an epistle meant to comfort a concerned mother. *I shall meet the duke tonight at dinner,* she wrote. *I will add to this letter after I have done so and tell you how I find him.*

The very thought of finding the duke set loose butterflies in her stomach. She hoped she would find him better than she remembered him.

At twenty minutes after six she inspected herself in the looking glass. She looked the perfect young lady, attired in a modest peach-colored gown with a square-cut neckline. She felt sure her wildly fluttering heart must be visible under the thin muslin and was amazed to see it wasn't. "I think I will do," she announced to Smythe, trying to sound calm and assured.

"Oh, yes, miss," agreed Smythe with loyal enthusiasm.

At twenty-five minutes after six, Celeste found herself following a footman across the flagged hallway and into an enormous room. Don't be nervous, she told herself. He is, after all, not really a beast.

The footman threw open heavy oak doors. Before her was a room larger than the ballroom at her home. A huge hearth took up a good portion of the wall opposite where she stood. Old tapestries depicting medieval scenes of jousting and hunting decorated the walls. And in the center of the room sat a table that could easily hold twenty but was set for two.

From the head of that table rose the Duke of St. Feylands. Although his body was still fit and trim, he had an old man's face, with deep lines cut alongside his mouth and faded blue eyes. He had a hawklike nose and a mane of dazzlingly white hair, both of which, combined with the proud angle of his head, made him look a most formidable host. Celeste blinked.

The footman handed her over to the butler, who announced her.

The duke came to her and she involuntarily took a step back. A look of irritation settled on his face. "Here now," he snapped in a gravelly voice. "I shan't be chasing you all about the dining hall. Stand still."

Celeste obeyed. In truth, she could do nothing else, for fear now kept her rooted where she stood. The Duke of St. Feylands came to stand before her and she attempted to drop him a curtsy. Unfortunately nerves made even such a simple and long-practiced gesture impossible. She overbalanced and tumbled to the floor.

"Give me your hand," came the terse command.

Her face ablaze, Celeste took the long hand offered her, conscious of the veins standing out, proclaiming more loudly than anything else the age of her benefactor, and found herself quickly pulled to her feet. "Forgive me," she murmured.

"I suppose you have become faint with hunger," he said in cynical tones. "Let us eat. I confess I am quite famished."

The footman held her chair for her and Celeste slid nervously onto it, thankful to be off her treacherous feet.

The butler proffered a soup tureen to the duke and he ladled himself out a bowlful. "So you are my Andromeda, sent to pay for your parents' sins," he observed casually.

"I am Celeste," she said hesitantly. Surely Papa had written to tell the duke her name.

St. Feylands raised his eyes heavenward and she wondered what she could have said to offend him.

"Andromeda was a young lady in Greek mythology, whose mother's pride displeased the gods. For punishment the woman was forced to send her to be devoured by a fierce monster."

Celeste could only manage a weak, "Oh." She looked at her soup and found she had little appetite for it.

The duke was regarding her with a cocked head. "Of course, in your case the offending parent is a father, rather than a mother, but I think the analogy works well nonetheless. I imagine that is a fairly accurate assessment of your situation, is it not? You are the one who was chosen to be offered up in exchange for my financial favors. Or was it the memory of my kind disposition and hospitality that brings you to me?"

Celeste knew not how to answer. Surely this was very rude to speak so openly before the servants. In fact, surely this was a most improper and unkind way to greet one's future wife. How would Mama respond? "This is most delicious soup," she said politely.

The duke grunted. "You lack nothing in deportment, at least," he said.

Celeste blushed and took a hasty sip of soup.

They ate in silence until the duke finished with his soup. He leaned back in his chair and regarded Celeste while the butler cleared away their dishes. "What accomplishments do you have?" he asked.

Celeste hesitated, searching her mind for some accomplishment that would please her benefactor.

"You do have accomplishments, don't you?" he prompted. "Or are you simply a pretty little ninnyhammer?"

"I am told I paint quite well," she managed.

"I shall see you are provided with the necessary materials," he said.

The next course arrived. The duke stabbed a mouthful of fish and asked, "Did you have admirers?"

"I am not yet out," said Celeste, shocked by his question.

"I didn't ask you if you were out. I asked if you had admirers."

The duke's voice was increasing in sharpness and Celeste found her nervousness equally increasing. Why was her host being so harsh with her? "I don't know," she said.

"Ha! Every woman knows when she has admirers.

You are taught to collect them," he said around a mouthful of fish.

Celeste felt an uncomfortable lump in her throat. How would she ever get through this meal?

"I suppose your papa sent you because you were the prettiest, because he thought you could turn me up sweet, get a little extra for your family. I have other heirs, you know, and feminine wiles won't work with me anymore. Your family will get no more from me than I have promised."

Celeste was blinking back tears now. Never in her life had her papa talked to her so! The duke was still talking, his gravelly voice raking over her raw nerves like claws. She sprang from her seat. "I pray you will excuse me," she said in a choked voice. "I find I have a headache and I think it best I retire."

"Retire?" he echoed.

Celeste picked up her skirt and ran out the door even as the duke was commanding her to return.

5

Celeste didn't stop running until she got to her room, where, panting and sobbing, she threw herself onto her bed. The duke was, indeed, a beast! Why, oh, why had she offered to come here? What would become of her? Her life as the Duchess of St. Feylands stretched before her like a prison sentence and her sobs turned to a wail.

She never heard the timid tapping on her door. Smythe's curly head peered in. "Miss?" she called softly. On seeing her mistress's distress, she rushed into the room. "Oh, miss. I just heard what happened to you at dinner. Oh, dear. Please don't cry so. You'll get the headache for certain."

Smythe's pleas were in vain, for Celeste continued to cry.

The little maid rushed to soak a handkerchief in lavender water and press it to Celeste's forehead. "Here, now," she soothed. "This will make you feel ever so much better."

"The only thing that will make me feel better is to leave this place," sobbed Celeste. "And that I cannot do." She raised her tearstained face to her maid. "He is so old. And so very frightening! How can I bear it?"

As Smythe had no answer to this question, it took a long time for her to calm her mistress and ready her for bed. When Celeste was at last attired in her nightgown, the girl left her reluctantly. "Will you be all right?" she asked.

Celeste nodded. "Yes. And thank you for your kindness to me." 'Tis most likely the only kindness I shall receive in this cold house, she thought miserably.

Exhausted by her emotions, Celeste went quickly to sleep. But it was a troubled sleep, filled with dreams in which she was stalked by a ferocious and ravening lion, and she awoke the next morning little rested from her seven hours in bed.

"Should you write your mama and papa and ask them to bring you home?" suggested Smythe as she combed out Celeste's hair.

Oh, wonderful, tempting thought! But, alas, impossible. "No," said Celeste. "My family is expecting me to do my duty and remain with the duke. What would happen to us all if I did not? Only Emily is engaged. The Earl of Umberland will never offer for Dorothea unless our family's fortunes are on the rise. And what would become of Mama and Papa if I threw away an opportunity to marry well? Where would they live? On what would they live?"

Smythe had no answer for those questions any more than did Celeste.

"No," continued Celeste. "I must remain. But I cannot remain under such conditions and keep my

The Wedding Deception 51

sanity. I shall have to do something to bring about a better understanding between the duke and myself."

But what? The duke was a bitter old bully. That much was obvious. What would Papa do?

Celeste continued to ponder that question as she went downstairs in search of breakfast. She sincerely hoped she wouldn't meet the duke, for as yet she had no idea what to say to him.

Breakfast, she discovered, was not served in the great dining hall, but in a smaller and more intimate dining parlor. And for that she was thankful, for that huge room had been terribly intimidating.

Why, she wondered, had she and the duke taken their first meal in that drafty old hall when this smaller and more cozy room would have served so much better? Had His Grace ordered their first meal served there simply to terrify and impress her? She would wager he had. What a beastly thing to do!

Celeste helped herself to eggs from the sideboard and fumed. Really! The Duke of St. Feylands's behavior the night before had been most unkind and undignified. The privilege of nobility came with certain responsibilities. Nobles were supposed to behave in a noble manner, to be kind to those less fortunate. The duke had certainly started out nobly enough by offering help to her family. But his behavior toward her on her first night in the castle had been anything but kind. Perhaps he resented her family's intrusion on his life. Perhaps Papa had written and asked for help and the duke had felt obliged to give it.

Well, what matter how it all came about? The duke *had* offered to help. If she could leave her home and travel to Gloucestershire and give her young life to a stranger, he could certainly show some civility!

Celeste's lovely face had taken on a variety of expressions as she waged her mental argument with the duke, and the footman present had been studying her with some interest. She finally became aware of his presence and blushed under his mystified gaze. "Is His Grace awake?" she asked.

"Yes, Miss Hart," he replied.

"Where will I find him?" she asked.

"In the library, miss."

Celeste rose. "Please show me to the library," she said.

The footman led the way, and with determination she marched after him. If she was doomed to spend the rest of her life in this wickedly enchanted castle, she would at least demand to be allowed to do so with dignity!

As if he'd been expecting her, she found the groom of chambers waiting by the door to that very room. He opened it for her, ushering her into the largest library she'd ever seen. It was easily three times the size of her father's library at home. For a moment she was distracted from her purpose, looking at the abundance of books with a greedy eye.

"Well," demanded a gruff voice, recalling Celeste to the purpose of her visit. "And what do you want so early this morning? Come to apologize for your behavior last night?"

Her legs began to tremble and her heart to beat erratically. The duke was, indeed, a terrifying person. But in spite of the trembling and palpitations, she stood her ground. "I certainly have not," she said. "But I have come to speak with you."

"Speak," said the duke.

"You succeeded admirably in terrifying me on my

first day here, and there is nothing I would like better than to leave this place. For I have never met a more beastly, overbearing man. But for my family's sake I must remain."

"Perhaps I shall not wish such a little harpy to remain in my house," countered the duke in his gravelly voice.

Celeste's chin went up and her eyes flashed. "I shall hold you to your offer. You are honor bound, Your Grace. And you are also honor bound to treat a guest in your home with kindness and not harsh words. I have done nothing to hurt you and, therefore, do not deserve such cruel treatment."

The duke bowed his head, as if in the presence of some painful memory. "We all receive cruelty we do not deserve at some time in our lives. You'd do well to remember that, child."

"I shall," she said, still angry. "And I hope that in the future you will remember your position, sir, and behave with the nobility such a position demands."

A corner of the duke's mouth twitched. "Noblesse oblige, eh? You are a most impertinent minx, aren't you?"

Horror at the enormity of what she had done engulfed Celeste and she bowed her head. "I am sorry to have spoken so unkindly," she said, "but in truth I could not for long bear such treatment as you gave me last night. I ask only that you give me the opportunity to prove myself worthy of your kindness. If I am unable to do so, then rail against me and I shall accept your scorn."

"Hmmph," said the duke.

This was not a satisfactory reply and Celeste remained where she stood, waiting.

"Very well," said the duke with a scowl. "I promise I shall not scold you at supper tonight. Does that satisfy you?"

Celeste beamed at him. "It does," she said.

"Well, then. Perhaps you will allow me to return to my work. Go sew or pick flowers or whatever it is young ladies like to do."

"This young lady likes to read," said Celeste.

The duke started to smile, but reined in the corners of his mouth.

Celeste cocked her head and grinned at him.

"Oh, very well. You may have the use of the library in the afternoon. After four o'clock."

"Thank you," she replied, the dimples in her cheeks mocking the primness of her voice. She turned to leave.

"Miss Hart," he called.

Celeste stopped.

"You may not think you have won some sort of victory this morning. You are here on my goodwill alone, and it would behoove you to cultivate it."

Celeste dropped him a curtsy. "Yes, Your Grace," she murmured, and left the room, still smiling. She had, indeed, won a victory, and they both knew it.

She went to her room and took up her letter to her mother. *Dear Mama*, she wrote. *The duke pretends to be an ogre, but underneath his gruff exterior I suspect he hides a kind heart. He has a most extensive library and has very kindly offered me the use of it.* Here she grinned triumphantly. *Mrs. Griffon, the housekeeper, will conduct me on a tour of the house this morning*, she continued. *I am most anxious to learn more about my new home.* And my host, she thought.

Half an hour later Celeste found herself in the

The Wedding Deception

gallery, looking at pictures of previous Dukes of St. Feylands and their duchesses. "Here is our duke," said Mrs. Griffon.

Celeste studied the portrait. The man in it was a good thirty years younger, his hair barely salted with white. His face was less lined, too. A very handsome man, actually, thought Celeste.

The duke's good looks weren't the thing that struck her the most about the picture, though. It was the look on his face. He had the look of a man content with his lot in life. The mouth, although not smiling, was not turned down. Instead it seemed to hover on the edge of a smile. But it was his eyes, she decided, that betrayed a happier state of mind. The eyes seemed to smile.

She searched the wall for a picture of his duchess. "Where is his wife?" she asked.

"He ordered her picture taken down," said Mrs. Griffon sadly.

Celeste looked at her, puzzled.

"The duke's is a very sad story. You see, he married a young French woman. She was very beautiful and he fell in love with her the moment he laid eyes on her. Alas, the two were very different. He was rather a sober man, and much older. She was a gay creature and, I'm sorry to say, shallow as a stream in August. It wasn't long after they married that they discovered they did not suit. She was easily bored, always in need of amusement, and happiest in London where she could attend society parties. He loved St. Feylands and enjoyed a quieter life. There were often quarrels."

Mrs. Griffon shook her head. "The poor man tried to make her happy. Took her to London every spring. In fact, that's where the trouble started. They attended some fancy party where she met a handsome, young cousin of hers, come to visit from France."

"Oh, dear," said Celeste, anticipating the outcome of the story.

Mrs. Griffon nodded. "I am afraid so. It broke the duke's heart. He was a different man after that. Quite bitter, I am afraid."

"And no wonder," said Celeste. "The poor man. How dreadful it must have been for him."

"He never allowed her name to be mentioned again. Told people she was dead. I believe she really is now."

Celeste shook her head.

Mrs. Griffon began to speak, but thought the better of it.

"Please," said Celeste. "I pray you, speak your mind with me."

"It is only that . . ." The housekeeper paused, as if searching for the right words. "I know the duke seems rather gruff at times. But he is a good man, really."

"I understand," said Celeste. And, indeed, she thought she did. Poor man. Small wonder, after what he had endured, he was so cynical and untrusting. She would have to be patient with him.

Dinner that night began more smoothly. Again, they ate in the Great Hall, but it didn't seem quite so intimidating as it had the night before. Her knowledge of the duke's painful past had broken the enchantment and taken terror from the room.

"You do not seem such a frightened little mouse tonight," commented the duke, dipping his spoon into his turtle soup.

"The house is not so strange to me," she said.

"Mrs. Griffon showed you about?"

Celeste nodded.

He took a spoonful of soup. "Did she show you the gallery?" he asked causally.

"Yes," she replied.

"Well?" he prompted.

"It is very fine," she said.

"I know it is very fine," he snapped. "What of the portraits?"

"They are very fine also," said Celeste, feeling a nervous twinge in her midsection. What was he getting at? What did he wish her to say? The duke was glaring at her and she felt a spark of anger catch fire somewhere inside her. "I must say the picture of you is a great deception," she snapped. "For in that you are not glaring."

"That picture is over thirty years old, painted long before I was married."

Celeste shrugged, giving a good imitation of her older sister. "I daresay that explains it," she said. "I suppose people are often happier in their youth." She must turn the conversation quickly. Perhaps the duke wished to know how much of his past his housekeeper had divulged to her. He was a proud man and she suspected he would not thank Mrs. Griffon for her efforts to paint him a sympathetic character. Celeste had no desire for his wrath to fall, either on herself or the housekeeper. "I very much enjoyed seeing the castle," she said quickly. "Especially the grounds."

"So. You think you might like it here."

"A lovely garden, a large library. Who would not?"

That had been the wrong thing to say. There had been one who had not. Celeste felt a hot blush burning her face and prattled on nervously about the many merits of the castle. She at last ran out of words and fell silent as the butler cleared away their dishes.

The duke sat studying her. "You are certainly a chatterbox," he observed.

Again, Celeste blushed. "I suppose I was tired of my own company and glad of someone to talk to tonight," she said.

The duke wondered aloud if discontent with one's own company was a common weakness among females.

"I wouldn't know," said Celeste. "I only know I grew up very much used to the society of others. Of course I had Mama and Papa and my sisters. And then there was always company, for my parents had many friends."

"Well, there will be no steady stream of visitors here, so don't be filling your silly little head with any such thoughts," said the duke.

Celeste blinked hard to push back the tears that threatened as a vision of her future as the Duchess of St. Feylands hovered frighteningly near. No friends, no visitors, and married to a man who would forever be growling at her.

"What is the matter now?" he demanded. "You look as if you are about to cry."

She would never let this horrid man think he had reduced her to tears! "I am afraid my head is beginning to ache. I am not yet recovered from the strain of my journey here. I think I shall retire immediately after dinner."

The duke shrugged. "Suit yourself."

The rest of their meal passed in silence, and when at last the butler decanted the duke's after-dinner port, she was thankful to make her escape. But instead of going to her room, she went out into the castle grounds to walk and think.

The grounds were, indeed, beautiful: lush lawn, a pleasure garden with every imaginable variety of flower and bush, a park. Celeste strolled across the lawn, making her way to the pleasure garden.

What was she to do? Mama had once said a wise woman could handle any man. However was she to handle the duke? She sighed. She was far too young for this mission. She should have allowed Papa to send Dorothea.

Celeste found a little stone bench nestled between some rosebushes and sat down to ponder her predicament. She knew she must be strong, for she sensed that the duke respected a strong woman. She remembered her small victory that morning when she had stood up to him. Yes, the duke would not be pleased with a mouse. It would also do him no harm to laugh occasionally. She must try to cheer him. But she knew she would have to tread carefully here, for his first wife had been a frivolous creature and had prejudiced him against any sort of levity. Celeste sighed. How could she possibly make him happy when he seemed determined to be bitter and miserable?

What to do, what to do? She gazed absently up at the castle, never seeing the figure of a man looking down on her from the French doors of the library.

The next day seemed to drag on forever. As a future bride and Duchess of St. Feylands, Celeste would have liked very much to learn how the castle was run, but as a guest she could hardly do so. And as a guest whose entertainment had not been considered in the least, she found herself with far too much time on her hands. She did explore the park, but found exploring by herself a rather lonely experience.

At home there had always been something to do or someone to talk with. "I need to employ myself," she announced to the hedgerow, and resolved to speak with the duke that very night about providing her with the materials for drawing as he'd promised.

Dinner was not such a strained affair this night. The duke was his usual grumpy self, but Celeste decided she would consider him no more than a naughty child and ignore his rude remarks. This proved to be a wise decision, for although it couldn't always take the sting from what he said, it did help her to keep from replying in kind or rushing from the room.

"I should like some drawing materials," she announced over dessert.

"Drawing?" echoed the duke. "Ah, yes. You did mention drawing as your one accomplishment," said His Grace cynically.

"I don't know whether I am accomplished or not," said Celeste, refusing to rise to the bait, "but I enjoy drawing and painting, and I wish to be occupied rather than idle."

"Very well. You shall have whatever you need. Tell Mrs. Griffon what you wish and she will send a footman into the village to purchase it for you."

Celeste smiled gratefully. "Thank you," she said.

"You are a guest in my house," said the duke, "not a prisoner. I wish you to be happy here."

Celeste stared at him. Could she have heard right? Kind words from the beast?

He frowned at her. "Do not look at me in such surprise. I am not a monster, you know."

Celeste grinned. "I am glad to know that," she said.

The Wedding Deception

"Hmmph," said the duke.

The dessert dishes were removed and the butler was setting a bowl of nuts before the duke. "I suppose you wish to run off to your room now," the old man growled.

Was that a challenge or a plea for her company? wondered Celeste. Well, she did not wish to be confined to her room every evening. "I shall await you in the drawing room," she announced, and left him to his port.

She had not been in the drawing room more than ten minutes when he joined her. "And now what would you like to do?" he demanded. "I suppose you mean to torture me by playing on the pianoforte and serenading me in a squeaky voice."

Such a typical Duke of St. Feylands remark, rude and to the point, thought Celeste. She smiled tolerantly and shook her head. "I do play a little, but I have no wish to torture you." She spied a chess set in the corner. "We could play chess," she suggested. "You do play chess?" Her voice was teasing.

"Of course I play chess," he snapped. "I was playing chess before you were born, young woman."

"Then you should make me an admirable opponent," said Celeste lightly, seating herself in front of the small table and surveying the pieces.

"Ha! I shall make you embarrassed," said the duke with relish, and joined her.

Before the hour was out, he had beaten her and was smiling triumphantly at her.

"You have won tonight, Your Grace," she teased, "but tomorrow you may not be so fortunate."

"Fortunate, is it?" he scoffed. "My dear child. That was skill. As for your playing, you do not look far enough ahead. Nor do you consider all the possible dangers around you."

"Tomorrow I shall," said Celeste. "You shall see."

The thought occurred to her that chess was not the only area where she did not consider all the possible dangers. She had certainly not carefully considered what awaited her here at the castle. Ah, well. What was the sense in dwelling in the past? She must play the game before her as best she could and not worry about whatever false moves lay behind her. She just hoped Dorothea was engaged to the Earl of Umberland by now. Then she wouldn't feel she'd sacrificed herself in vain.

She looked up to find the duke regarding her, but not unkindly. "Why don't you sing something for me?" he suggested. "Perhaps your voice is not so painfully squeaky as I have imagined it to be."

"Very well," she said, and went to the pianoforte, thinking that perhaps the beast was not so awful as she'd thought. Perhaps he might be tamed.

6

THE FOLLOWING NIGHT they again played chess. Dinner had been a more genial affair, and other than the duke once berating Celeste for a stupid chess move, the evening went smoothly as well. Once again, he won their game, but it took him longer to do so, a fact she proudly pointed out to him.

"Save your bragging for the day you beat me," he said.

She wasn't intimidated. "It will come," she predicted. "For I am watching you carefully. And I am learning."

He conceded this with a nod. "That you are. And I'll say this for you, you are a quick study."

Celeste smiled. She knew this was all the praise she'd get and she was well pleased with it.

The supper tray was brought in. The duke watched her help herself to cheese and a small cake. "Good grief, girl. Is that all you are having? You barely ate any dinner. How do you expect to stay alive when you eat like a bird?"

"My sister Dorothea always said I was a pig," said Celeste.

A bushy, white eyebrow shot up. "Did your sister correct you a great deal?" asked His Grace.

"Yes, but I suppose that is how older sisters are," said Celeste. "Always bullying their younger sisters."

"And your other sister. There was another, was there not? Did she bully you also?"

Celeste shrugged. "Occasionally. Of course, I know both Emily and Dorothea felt that Mama and Papa allowed me more freedom than they had allowed them at my age. I suppose that knowledge did not always dispose them toward tolerance."

"And what freedom was that?" prompted the duke.

"It was not so very much, really," said Celeste. "I was allowed to attend small dinner parties, and to join the grown-ups when visitors came to the house."

"And did you enjoy those occasions?"

"Oh, yes. For the most part." She shrugged. "Some of my sisters' friends were not so friendly."

"The ladies?" guessed the duke.

Celeste nodded.

The duke cut off a generous helping of pheasant and set it on her plate. "What did your oldest sister say when offered a chance to come here?" he asked.

Celeste felt the unwelcome warmth of a blush on her cheeks and found a sudden interest in the contents of her plate. "Of course she would have loved to come," she began.

"As eldest, she should have come," said His Grace.

"She was as good as engaged to the Earl of Umberland."

The Wedding Deception

"That is not what I heard. I heard he made himself scarce after your family's misfortune."

Celeste bit her lip. She felt the duke's keen eyes on her and dared not look up.

"Are your sisters beautiful?" he asked casually.

Celeste heard the scrape of utensil on plate and felt the danger was past. She looked up and saw that the duke was, indeed, occupied with his supper. "Yes, they are," she replied.

"Are they as beautiful as you?" he asked.

"I am not beautiful," she said.

"Come now," he scolded. "No fishing for compliments."

"But I wasn't," protested Celeste.

The duke stared at her, a look of perturbation on his face. "Who told you that you are not beautiful?" he demanded.

"It is just something I've known for a long time," she said. "Dorothea and Emily are the ones with all the suitors."

"Of course they have many suitors," said the duke. "They are—how did you put it—out. You are not. Did their suitors talk with you?"

"Naturally they talked with me," said Celeste. "They were all very kind."

"I am sure they were," murmured His Grace. He set down his plate. "You will, most likely, not wish to hear this, for we never wish to hear ill of our close relations, but your sisters sound to me like selfish young ladies."

Celeste opened her mouth to defend her sisters and realized she couldn't, for what the duke said was true.

"You may be grateful for the service they have done you," he said.

Celeste looked questioningly at him.

"Their selfishness was the chisel which carved your humility," he said. He sighed. "Would that I had allowed the faults of others to work so well on me. Perhaps bitterness is a privilege of the old."

"Surely bitterness can be no privilege," argued Celeste, not seeing the irony behind the words. "It must be a curse, for it makes all of life unpalatable."

The duke sat regarding her. "Well said," he said at last. "You are an unusually intelligent woman. Your father chose well in sending you to me. Perhaps this old man may yet taste the sweet waters of happiness." He set aside his plate and sighed again, a great, noisy sigh. "I am tired. I think I shall seek my bed."

"I, too," said Celeste. And before he could rise, she bent over him and placed a kiss on his forehead.

"Go on with you now," he growled. "Don't be playing those female tricks off on me."

But she could tell by the tone of his voice that his protest was halfhearted, and for the first time since her arrival at St. Feylands she went to bed feeling almost content with her fate.

As the days passed, Celeste began to feel more comfortable in her new home. She still found the duke's crusty behavior irritating, but she no longer found it unnerving. Nor was his quickness to speak his opinions.

On her third day at the castle he found her in the library, helping herself from a set of novels, which she supposed must have been bought for the first duchess. "You would do better to read Homer or Ovid than that frippery stuff," he told her. "What you need is something to exercise your mind." He took a book from the library shelf and piled it on top of the two novels she held in her arms. "There," he said, satisfied. "Have your dessert. But have something that is good for you as well."

"Yes, Your Grace," she replied meekly, and thought to herself, I hope you may not mind, but I intend to have my dessert first.

They played chess again that evening, he instructing her all the while with broad hints and subtle warnings.

When he had finally beaten her, she felt far from discouraged. "I almost had you twice tonight," she said. "I warn you, you are in imminent danger of losing to me before the week is out."

"I still have a few tricks left," he said. "But I confess that soon I shall have to quit toying with you and play in earnest."

Celeste was insulted. "I thought you were playing in earnest," she said.

"Tomorrow night I shall show you what it is to play in earnest," he said in ominous tones. "Now," he began, dismissing the subject of chess, "tell me more about your family."

"What would you like me to tell you?"

"Whatever you wish," he said.

Celeste complied. She told him of her family's pretty house on the Thames, of the lovely ladies who came to visit her mother, of picking strawberries every June. "We were very happy," she concluded.

"Until your father lost his fortune," added the duke.

Celeste blinked back tears.

"Why do you think he gambled so?"

"My father never gambled," she said, quick to defend her papa.

"Of course he did," argued the duke. "Don't delude

yourself, girl. The 'change can be as big a gamble as any card game. In fact, it is the biggest game of chance of them all. Why do you think he risked security for riches?"

"I don't know," said Celeste, stunned. "I never really thought about it."

"Did you and your sisters and mama complain of your life?"

"Why, no!" exclaimed Celeste. "Mama would never do such a thing. And what reason would Dorothea and Emily have to complain?"

The duke shrugged. "Not enough fine ball gowns? A carriage less fine than those of the grand ladies they met in London ballrooms?"

"Oh, sometimes my sisters bemoaned the fact that we did not have so much as this or that family, but surely Papa would not listen to such idle complaints."

"What is an idle complaint to a woman can seem like a severe criticism to a man."

The duke's face took on a faraway look and Celeste wondered if he was watching some painful scene from his past. What idle complaints had his pretty young bride made to hurt his pride? She supposed she'd probably never know. But she did know she'd be careful not to complain, for although she was no longer nervous in his company, she knew her temperamental host's disposition and had no desire to provoke him.

Celeste's first week at St. Feylands was undisturbed by visitors, and although she found it a little lonely, she didn't find it upsettingly so. The duke was as good as his word and sent a servant to the village to produce some drawing materials for her: chalk, watercolors, and paper. And she amused herself by sitting in the pleasure garden after breakfast each morning and painting.

The only thing that upset her the rest of her first week at the castle was the fact that she received no letter from home. Every day she checked the silver salver on the table in the entry hall and found it void of any correspondence for her.

The young footman, Charles, always tried to encourage her. "Perhaps tomorrow, Miss Hart," he'd say, and she'd smile bravely and nod her head, unable to speak for the lump in her throat.

But once over her disappointment, Celeste usually found enough to occupy herself in the huge, rambling castle, where there was still much to explore. And the duke had taken to having her accompany him when he rode out to visit various tenants on the estate. Although she was a modest horsewoman (a fault that did not please His Grace), she enjoyed being out in the fresh air and having some contact with other people.

On Sunday he took her to church in the village, where they sat in the St. Feylands pew, to the awe and delight of the other worshipers.

Celeste would have enjoyed this event much more if the duke hadn't swooped her off into his carriage before the rector could say more than a quick word of welcome.

"Why are you pouting?" he demanded as they drove off.

"I am not pouting," said Celeste stiffly, although she knew in truth that she had been.

"Oh, yes, you are," he said. "I suppose you would have liked to stand on the church doorstep half the morning with all the villagers gaping at us, and with the squire's wife bearing down on us like a ship in full sail."

"Well, I would have liked to have said more than good morning to the rector," admitted Celeste. "One would have thought the way you dragged me away that you feared we should catch some sort of plague."

"Hmmph," said the duke.

"Why did we leave so quickly?" asked Celeste.

"Because the rector is a toad-eater," he snapped. "Just as are the squire and his wife. And I detest being toadied to."

"Hmmph," said Celeste.

It wasn't until the middle of the following week that, on checking the silver salver, Celeste found a letter in her mother's handwriting.

Hugging it to her, she hurried out to the pleasure garden to enjoy her treat in the sunshine. *My dearest daughter,* she read. *I hope this letter finds you well. Please write us soon and tell us how you find the duke. I hope you are not too terribly homesick.* She has not yet gotten my letter, thought Celeste. It was a somewhat sad thought. She had always been so close to her mother, and this herky-jerky means of communication that was the mail coach seemed less than satisfactory.

But she consoled herself with the fact that, perhaps, even as she was reading her mother's letter that good woman had her daughter's missive on her lap and was perusing her account of life at St. Feylands.

Celeste read on. *I am afraid that we have received some rather disheartening news regarding Dorothea's hopes. There was an announcement in the* Gazette *earlier this week. The Earl of Umberland is now engaged to another young lady. It is a pity he could not have waited, but I have tried to console Dorothea by telling her that the earl could not have been very much in love with her to offer so quickly for another, and that a man more worthy of her affections will surely come along. Of course, when one is experiencing a broken heart, such words are of little comfort, as Dorothea was quick to inform me.*

Celeste set the letter in her lap and stared off into the distance. She had left her home to marry an old man so her sister could marry well. Now there was to be no marriage. "So it was all for naught," she said, and sighed.

"Sad news?" came a voice from behind her.

Celeste jumped. "Oh, Your Grace! How you startled me."

The duke approached the stone bench. "Do I intrude?" he asked.

Only a week ago he would never have bothered to ask, thought Celeste. She shook off her melancholy as best she could and rewarded her benefactor with a smile. She patted the seat beside her. "By all means, join me," she said.

"So you have finally heard from you family," he observed.

She nodded. "It would appear that poor Dorothea's hopes have been dashed. The Earl of Umberland has offered for another."

The duke regarded her solemnly. "She is free, then, to take your place."

His words surprised her. But not so much as the twinge of hurt she felt at hearing them. "Do you wish me gone, then?"

"Of course I don't wish you gone," he snapped. "I should hate to have to deal with the foibles of yet another Hart daughter." He looked off, suddenly intent on surveying the castle. "Would you wish to leave?"

Celeste thought about this. Her first day at St. Feylands she would have snapped at such an offer. But now? "I am not sure," she said slowly, thinking out loud. "Of course I miss Mama and Papa very much, but I don't miss Emily so very much, and I don't miss Dorothea in the least. I am, in fact, rather happy here. And someone must stay."

"Ah, yes," said the duke. "Someone must stay." He regarded her profile. "The company of an old man is not much for a young girl," he said.

Celeste smiled teasingly at him. "Even when you are not good company, your books are."

"Vixen," he said. "Well, here is some news which should do your frivolous little heart good. We have a houseguest coming."

Celeste clapped her hands. "Company!" she cried. "Now I am very glad, indeed, I am staying," she teased.

"He will arrive on Saturday and stay through Tuesday," continued the duke.

"Who is this person?"

"A relative of mine, the Earl of Greenfield. A pesky fellow, really. And handsome. All the ladies swoon for him, I hear. Of course the fact that he has both title and fortune may be the cause for most of the swooning. At any rate you may meet him and judge for yourself."

"Why does he come?" asked Celeste.

"Because he is a relative," replied the duke gruffly. "One can hardly ignore one's relations. As you should well know."

"Yes, I suppose you are right," agreed Celeste,

ignoring his tone of voice as well as the fact they were hardly related.

"Of course," added the duke, "I am sure he has also come to see you."

"Me?"

"Most like he has a great curiosity to see the woman to whom I have offered the opportunity to become the future Duchess of St. Feylands."

"*If* she proves suitable," Celeste reminded him.

"And 'tis early days still," said His Grace. "So don't go planning your bride clothes yet."

Celeste hid a smile. After several days in the duke's company she was beginning to recognize bluster when she heard it.

The duke slapped his hands on his knees and pushed himself up from the bench. "I must get back inside," he said. "Some people may have no better use for their time than to sit in the sunshine, but I have work to do."

"I shall accompany you inside," Celeste announced, also rising. "I must confer with Cook about what to serve our guest."

The duke muttered something about interfering young ladies who poked their noses where there was no need to go poking them, and she took his arm and walked with him into the castle.

After the best possible meals to please someone so rare as a visitor had been decided, Celeste wandered off to while away an hour looking at the portraits in the gallery. And to try and imagine what the Earl of Greenfield might look like. If the earl was related to the duke, would he look like His Grace?

She had been unable to get much information out of Mrs. Griffon regarding the mysterious earl, other than the fact that he was next in line for the succession. Mrs. Griffon had been able to assure her, however, that he was a very amiable man of nearly thirty years, and that he was, indeed, as handsome as the duke had said.

A man whom ladies swooned over, thought Celeste, remembering the duke's words. Would she swoon over him?

7

Celeste watched from the window Saturday afternoon as a crested carriage pulled to a stop in front of the castle. A footman hopped from it to let down the steps and out came the most handsome man Celeste had ever seen. "He is even more handsome than Edward Finch," she reported to Smythe, who joined her and peeped over her shoulder.

"Oh, my," was all Smythe could say.

The Earl of Greenfield had dark, thick hair and equally thick, dark eyebrows over very fine blue eyes. His nose was straight, his chin strong, and his shoulders broad. And best of all, he wore a smile on his face. He threw open his arms in a gesture of greeting and strode up the steps and out of sight.

Celeste turned from the window and pondered what she had just seen. The earl had been about to embrace someone, and that someone had to be the duke. It seemed almost odd to think of anyone being so delighted to see her crotchety groom-to-be that he would rush to embrace him. But it was certainly comforting. At least the duke had someone in his life who cared. They would not live as complete hermits.

Celeste wondered if she should go belowstairs to meet their guest or wait to be summoned. She was anxious to meet the fine-looking gentleman, but she wasn't anxious to incur the duke's wrath.

Smythe timidly echoed her thoughts. "Do you think you should go down and welcome him, miss?"

"I am sure the duke will send for me soon enough," said Celeste, trying to sound calm.

Half an hour later there was a knock at Celeste's sitting-room door. Smythe answered it. It was a footman. The duke had at last summoned her.

She nervously smoothed out her gown, and Smythe made one last, unnecessary adjustment to her hair ribbon, then she went downstairs to the drawing room to meet the Earl of Greenfield.

She entered the drawing room and he stood. She caught her breath. He was even more handsome up close. So very broad-shouldered, such blue eyes, such a kind smile. Prince Charming, she thought, remembering her nursery days. Embarrassed by such a fanciful thought, she lowered her eyes.

"This is Miss Hart," the duke was saying.

The earl came forward and she gave him her hand. What an odd thrill ran through her as he took it! She never felt like this when Papa took her hand, or the duke, or even Edward Finch. "It is a pleasure," he said. "I heard of your coming and have been most anxious to meet you. The duke told me your family's sad story. Please allow me to offer my condolences."

Celeste sent a quick reproachful look at the duke.

How could he have been so unkind as to bandy about her family's misfortune?

"I hope the Hart family's fortunes have begun to reverse themselves?" the earl continued.

Celeste smiled at him. "They have, mainly due to the duke's kindness." Here again, she looked at the duke. "I suppose His Grace has told you of his kind offer." Most likely he had. He seemed to have told the earl everything else about them!

The earl nodded and, as if he had read her mind, said, "He has, and you must not reproach him for doing so. As next in line for the title, I am sure he felt I had a right to know." He turned to the duke. "Isn't that so, sir?"

"Whether that's so or not is no business of Miss Hart's," said the duke crossly. "Now sit down, both of you."

The two obeyed, and as they did so the butler made his appearance with tea and cakes, and Celeste set about pouring.

She tried to steal another look at the handsome man, but on finding his gaze on her, nervously directed her attention to her teacup. The earl tried to draw her out. How was she enjoying her stay at St. Feylands? What did she find to amuse herself with only the duke to entertain her?

Celeste, normally a friendly and unaffected young lady, found herself oddly tongue-tied, answering the earl's first question with a monosyllable.

As she hesitated over the second question the duke broke in, "Well, don't just sit there like a simpleton, girl. Say something."

"How can she say anything with you bellering at her?" scolded the young man. He turned kindly to

Celeste. "I hope you are finding something to amuse you in spite of the obvious rudeness of your host," he said.

"Oh, yes," said Celeste. "And he is not so very rude sometimes," she added, defending the duke.

The earl chuckled. "What have you done to cause the young lady to spring to your undeserved defense?" he teased the duke.

"I have taught her to play a far better game of chess than you shall ever play."

The earl was amazed. "No!"

The duke nodded, and Celeste smiled, proud of her small accomplishment.

"Of course she still an indifferent horsewoman," the duke continued. "In spite of my efforts to improve her."

Again the earl turned to Celeste. "Are you?" he asked.

She nodded and bit her lip. "I am afraid I am much too timid."

"I should be timid also, if I had such a fierce old bird screeching at me," said the earl in a mock whisper.

Celeste was surprised that the young man could talk so disrespectfully and suffer no recriminations. But, she concluded, it was as she had suspected, the duke respected those who had the courage to stand up to him.

"I would be delighted to work with you on improving your horsemanship, Miss Hart," the earl offered.

Celeste blushingly thanked him for his kindness and took refuge behind her teacup. Why the handsome man was having such an effect on her she had no idea, for she had never felt so self-conscious with any of the young men who visited her father's house.

The Wedding Deception 79

She endured another twenty minutes before excusing herself, saying she would rest awhile before dinner. The gentleman stood and bowed her out and she rushed from the room.

They settled back down and the younger man eyed the older. "She seems a sweet young lady," he said. "And I vow I've never seen one more beautiful. She definitely puts the sisters in the shade."

"From what I can tell there is no comparison in character either," said the duke.

The young man fidgeted with is quizzing glass. "Are you sure you wish to continue with this scheme?" he asked at last.

"I do," said the earl. "Why not kill two birds with one stone? Help these unfortunate relations, who have remembered me—and only in their hour of need—and find a woman suitable to be Duchess of St. Feylands."

"Hart could have sent one of the other daughters, you know," said Greenfield.

The duke grinned at him. "But he did not, did he? And from everything you told me I knew he would not. The one daughter engaged, the other hoping to catch Umberland—who else was there left to send but the little beauty who is already the talk of the ton?"

The earl looked toward the door, as if still seeing the girl there. "She seems a sweet little thing."

"She does," agreed the duke, "but let her prove herself."

"It would seem she already has."

"She's barely been here two weeks. That is hardly enough time in which to know a woman's name, let alone her character. Oh, the girl seems a noble one, I grant you. But society chits all have a mask they wear when they hunt a husband. And it takes time for the mask to slip. You promised silence. Do not break that promise, Arthur."

"Why I was ever mad enough to agree to such a deception I'll never know," said the earl.

"You bowed to a wiser head. Believe me, boy. I've been deceived before, and 'tis no pleasant experience."

"No, not deceived," began the younger man, but the duke cut him off with a raised hand.

"I know your feelings on this subject, and you know mine. There is no sense in engaging in painful discussion. Let us be satisfied to agree that I act with the best of motives."

The younger man acquiesced with a nod of the head.

Upstairs Celeste and her maid were discussing the earl as thoroughly as he and the duke had been discussing her. "He is so well mannered," Celeste reported. "Not at all like the duke. Of course that is not to say he does not speak his mind. But he does so in the kindest of ways, so that one does not mind at all."

"And is he as handsome close up as he was from the window?" asked Smythe.

"Even more so. I vow, I have never seen a man so handsome." Celeste's smile faded. "What is the sense in noticing how handsome he is? I am already as good as betrothed."

Smythe's position prevented her from voicing an opinion on such a sad state of affairs, but it didn't forbid her from giving her mistress a sympathetic look.

Celeste smiled at her. "The duke is not so very bad,"

she said with a fatalistic shrug. "Oh, I admit he can be rather an old crosspatch at times. But really, he is not so often cross with me anymore, and I believe he is rather fond of me."

Smythe nodded loyally, ready to agree to anything Celeste said.

"And I must never forget the great kindness he does my family," Celeste added.

She sighed and wished her father had waited just one more year to lose his fortune. After she had come out. Perhaps, then, she might have met the Earl of Greenfield at a London party. Perhaps they would have fallen in love. Perhaps, when he'd heard of her family's troubles, he would have offered for her. . . .

"Perhaps you would care to wear the cream-colored silk gown your mama gave you," Smythe was suggesting.

Celeste turned her back on the tantalizing vision and turned her attention to dressing for dinner.

Dinner was a positively gay affair. The earl enjoyed everything, from the turbot to the syllabub. "And the dinner I did not enjoy half so much as the charming company in which I ate it," he said, with an admiring glance for Celeste. "I must say, it is a pleasant change from having to eat dinner with only this old rogue for company, which is my usual fate when I visit."

"I never heard you complain before," grumped the duke. "Maybe you'll not find Celeste's company so charming after she annihilates you at the chessboard."

"Ah, yes," said the earl, leaning back in his seat. "The duke's discovery."

"She will give you a humbling you richly deserve," boasted the duke.

The earl cocked his head and studied Celeste. "Will you?" he asked.

She smiled. "I hope so," she said. "For I am very fond of winning."

The two men laughed and she excused herself and left them to their port.

She did, indeed, beat the earl at chess. "But that is because I was not paying proper attention," he said.

"You weren't?" Celeste was shocked.

"With such a lovely creature sitting opposite me? How could I?" Celeste blushed and he chuckled. "No. That is not fair. I belittle your victory with such frivolous statements. You won fair and square, and I must admit, you are, indeed a very good player. I shall have to demand you give me another chance. Perhaps next time I may at least go down with more of a fight."

"Hmmph. You should have paid more attention to my instructions as a lad," commented the duke.

"I had rather receive instructions from Miss Hart," said the earl, and gave Celeste a wink.

She blushed. The earl said the most embarrassing things! Was he flirting with her? And what should she do? Should she flutter her eyelashes at him as she'd seen Em do with Mr. Swineburn? She smiled and blinked rapidly.

"What the devil's the matter with you?" demanded the duke. "Have you got something in your eye?"

Celeste blushed furiously. "No," she said, and lowered her gaze.

"Well, I wouldn't be surprised if she had tears in 'em now," the earl told him. "Here now, you mustn't mind the duke," he said to Celeste.

"Hmmph," said the duke.

"Most of the time I don't," murmured Celeste.

The Wedding Deception

"There's a fine thing to say about your host," said the duke irritably.

"Good girl," approved Greenfield. "You seem a very bright young lady, and I suppose by now you have learned that while he has a nasty bark, our relation's bite is little to be feared."

"Here now," protested his grace. "I refuse to be spoken of as though I weren't here. And I'll thank you not to speak of the head of this house as though he were some great, hairy dog."

Celeste bit back a giggle. How very pleasant it was to have company. And such very good company!

By midnight she could keep her eyes open no longer.

"Find your bed, child," said the duke. "You look more dead than alive."

Celeste was happy to obey. Unashamed, she kissed the old man's cheek, then gave her hand to the earl.

He took it and planted a kiss on it, which sent an unexpected shiver through her and made the blood rush to her face. Confused and frightened by her body's strange reaction, she snatched her hand away. Then, thoroughly embarrassed by her gauche behavior, she whispered good night and fled the room, the duke's amused chuckle echoing in her ear.

"Oh, Smythe," she moaned, once inside the safety of her bedchamber, "I wish I had had my London season. I don't know how to behave like a lady."

"Oh, no, miss," protested Smythe. "Everyone in the whole household says what a nice young lady you are, so kind, so pretty . . ."

"So graceless," added Celeste miserably. "The earl kissed my hand just now. And what did I do, but turn red as a beet and snatch my hand away?" She covered her face, trying to blot out the image. "Oh, I must have looked such a fool."

"What did the earl do?" asked Smythe.

"He just smiled at me. Oh! I was so embarrassed."

"By tomorrow he will have forgotten," predicted Smythe.

"But I won't have," said Celeste.

And her own gauche behavior wasn't all she wouldn't be able to forget. She knew the memory of his lips brushing her hand would haunt her for a long time. Disloyal heart! Don't think about the earl, she scolded. It is the duke you must marry.

The next morning she met the earl at breakfast. Just the sight of him started her feelings tumbling again and brought a guilty flush to her cheeks.

If he noticed it, however, he was too much a gentleman to comment. Instead he asked her how she slept, and other innocuous questions, until she once more felt quite comfortable in his presence.

The duke joined them, and after breakfast they went to church to set the proper example for the villagers and estate tenants.

There was much gawking as the three took their places in the family pew. And who wouldn't gawk, thought Celeste, with such a handsome man as the Earl of Greenfield in their presence.

All the men present were scrubbed and in their Sunday best, including a young man sitting next to the squire, whom Celeste judged to be his son. He was broad and strong looking with fair skin and fine features, but compared with the earl he looked a peasant. But then, what man could possibly hope to compare with the Earl of Greenfield, with his perfect features and his fine clothes and immaculate grooming?

After the services the earl was quick to commend the rector on a fine sermon as they stood on the front-porch step.

"Thank you, Your Lordship," said the rector. "And may I say what a pleasure it is to see you back among us?"

"You may," said the duke, taking Celeste by the arm and leading her away. "And now you may say good-bye. Fine sermon, by the way," he called over his shoulder.

The earl stayed a moment longer, talking with the rector, then ran after them, easily catching up with them at the carriage.

"Fine fellow," he commented as the duke handed Celeste up.

"He seems very nice," said Celeste. "I should so have liked to stay a moment longer," she added wistfully.

"Nonsense," said the duke briskly. "What else would you possibly have to say to the fellow? You have nothing in common."

"I should tell him what a pretty little church that is," began Celeste.

"Very well. You may tell him that next week."

"I should also offer to stitch him a new altar cloth," she continued.

"Very well. You may offer next week," said the duke.

"You will allow me to linger long enough to do so?"

"Of course," said the duke in a voice that plainly told her she was being absurd.

When they arrived home, the duke announced that

he had a great desire to be left in peace and advised his guests to take themselves off somewhere and find something to amuse them until dinner was served.

Greenfield turned to Celeste. "Have you seen much of the surrounding countryside?"

"A little," said Celeste. "I have been around the estate with the duke."

"Perhaps you would fancy a ride through the Cotswolds?"

"I am not a very good horsewoman," Celeste reminded him.

"Since we are not riding to hounds, it won't matter," said Greenfield pleasantly, and an hour later she found herself trotting along beside him down a country lane.

"I hope you are not allowing the duke to bully you too much," he said casually.

Celeste recalled her early interview with His Grace. She smiled and shook her head.

"Do you think you could be happy here?" he continued.

Was that quite a proper question to ask someone in her position? wondered Celeste. "I have enjoyed my stay very much," she hedged.

"And the duke?" he asked. "Do you enjoy him?"

Surely this was most improper! And how to answer? She had thought herself happy enough with the duke until the Earl of Greenfield had come. "The duke has been very kind to me," she said. "And I have grown quite fond of him."

They entered the woods and Celeste was reminded of the fairy tales of her childhood. As she looked around her she thought she could almost see wicked witches hiding behind trees. She remembered the tale Miss

Pringle used to tell of the beautiful Snow White, and how the huntsman had been commissioned to take her into the deep woods and kill her. Snow White had survived her ordeal and been rewarded with a happy ending.

Did anyone who lived outside the pages of a book live happily ever after? she wondered, and then scolded herself for such a selfish, ungrateful thought. Of course they did! Thanks to the duke, her family would.

"Tuppence for your thoughts," said Greenfield.

Celeste was startled out of her reverie. She shook her head and smiled. "They were rather silly thoughts, I am afraid."

"Then I should, indeed, like to hear them," he said encouragingly.

"I was just remembering the fairy tales of my childhood. So many of them took place in woods such as these."

"Do you believe in fairy tales?" asked Greenfield lightly.

"No," said Celeste sadly.

"Do you, at least, believe in happy endings?" he continued.

Celeste looked ahead to the ending in store for her. Well, life with the duke would certainly be happier than it would be as a spinster, cooped up in a small cottage with Dorothea. "Yes," she said slowly. "I believe everyone can find some happiness in life. Don't you?"

"Oh, yes," he said enthusiastically. He smiled at her. "I have certainly found more than my fair share this afternoon."

Celeste lowered her gaze and smiled. The earl

obviously enjoyed her company. It was a lovely day. What more could she ask? And then, before her heart could tell her, she answered sternly, nothing.

They rode back to the castle, bantering as though they had been friends for a very long time. The earl asked her questions about her family, and as she told him of her life she revealed more about herself than she realized.

"You are a very unusual young lady," said the earl at last.

Celeste looked at him in surprise. "Why, there is nothing so very unusual about me," she said.

"Very few young women would embark on such an adventure as you have to help their family, I assure you," said Greenfield.

"I find that very difficult to believe," said Celeste.

He smiled. "I am sure you do," he said.

They arrived back at the castle, and the earl sprang from his horse and ran to help her down. Again, she felt that pleasantly unnerving shiver as his hands closed around her waist to swing her down, and she blushed. "You needn't help me, Your Lordship. I could have easily used the mounting block."

Slowly, as if reluctant to let her go, the earl removed his hands. He smiled down at her. "Ah, yes. But this is a much more pleasant way to dismount. Wouldn't you agree?"

In spite of her embarrassment and confusion, she returned his gaze. "Yes, I believe I would," she said. Then, truly mortified by her boldness, she excused herself and ran off into the castle.

All that evening she felt the earl's admiring eyes on her and found she liked it very much. And when it came time to bid the gentlemen good night, she found

The Wedding Deception

herself hoping the earl would, again, kiss her hand. He did not disappoint her, and she went to bed wrapped in a warm gauzy happiness. Life at St. Feylands was becoming most enjoyable!

The following morning the duke took the earl out to view the estate. Celeste would like to have gone, too, but since no one invited her, she settled for spending her morning in the pleasure garden, painting.

After her enjoyment in the company of the earl, the solitude of the garden felt more like loneliness. How the time stretched when one was by oneself!

Her painting didn't hold the attraction for her it usually did, and she at last gave up trying to content her restless heart with brush and colors and went inside.

After putting away her paints, she headed for the library, looking for a book to occupy her mind. The door was open a crack, as though someone had entered and not thought to close it. Where was the groom of chambers? It seemed he was always standing about, waiting to open doors for people.

Curiosity made Celeste's steps slow. The sound of voices drifted out to her and she drew near the door.

She recognized the Earl of Greenfield's voice. "This is most unfair," he was saying. "You should tell her."

"Did we not just discuss this?" snapped the duke impatiently. "I have told her all she needs to know for the present. And I absolutely forbid you to say anything. Is that clear, Arthur?"

There was a long silence. "I have fallen in love with the girl," said the earl.

"Bah," spat the duke. "In two days' time? Don't be ridiculous."

"I am not being ridiculous," replied the earl. "You know I have seen enough young ladies to know a rare one when I see her, and may I remind you that I am certainly old enough—"

"You are old enough to do a great many things," interrupted the duke. "But you are not yet in my shoes!"

The duke's voice was rising. Even as Celeste backed away the duke's angry words followed her, "I am still head of this household and I forbid you—" She stopped her ears and ran off down the hall, tears running from her eyes.

The duke wanted her for himself, that much was plain. He'd as much as told the Earl of Greenfield so.

I don't believe in happy endings, thought Celeste bitterly. Not at all.

8

At dinner it was hard for Celeste to behave as though she had never heard the conversation between her benefactor and his guest. She tried to smile and appear as if nothing was wrong, but she knew her eyes made that smile a lie. The earl was leaving in the morning, a fact that was, in itself, sad. But knowing the duke would never let him marry her was grief itself.

"You seem pensive tonight," ventured the earl.

"I am thinking how much we shall miss you," she said.

The duke glared at her from the head of the table. "Young women these days are much too bold," he observed.

Celeste blushed and lowered her eyes to her plate. A fine piece of turbot sat on it, but she couldn't bring herself to put so much as a bite of the thing in her mouth.

"I suppose you'll wish to come for another visit before the summer's out," the duke was saying.

The tone of his voice was as begrudging as his words, but Lord Greenfield took no offense. "Naturally," he said. "I should hate to be deprived of the opportunity to see Miss Hart again before she returns to her mother and father." He cocked his head and smiled teasingly at Celeste. "Should you be glad to see me again, Miss Hart?" he asked.

How can he banter so, when he knows the duke will never let him have me? wondered Celeste miserably. Perhaps he thinks to persuade the duke into letting him court me. Perhaps he has dreams of an elopement.

This sounded romantic, indeed, except Celeste was sure she'd heard somewhere that elopements weren't quite the thing. And besides, she'd given her word she'd marry the duke. She knew that as her husband he had the power to help her family, and as a loyal daughter she owed it to them to act in their best interests. Who knew what kind of fortune, if any, the Earl of Greenfield had? Maybe he was like Dorothea's Earl of Umberland, tilted but lacking in money.

Oh, but he was so handome! There he sat, the embodiment of every girl's dream with that glossy dark hair and that perfect, smiling face. And such broad shoulders!

"Well, answer girl! Are you dumb?"

The duke's harsh words cut into her thoughts and she felt her face go warm. "I am sorry. What were you saying?"

"I asked if you would like to see me again," said the earl.

This time the light tone was gone and Greenfield

was looking at her as if the fate of the world rested on her answer.

She should say something clever and flirtatious, she knew. It was what Dorothea or Emily would have done. Instead she met the earl's look with one equally sober. "I should very much like to see you again, Your Lordship," she said.

"Hmmph," grunted the duke, but the earl was grinning widely.

The gentlemen didn't linger long over their port. They joined Celeste in the drawing room almost immediately.

"I have not yet had the pleasure of hearing you sing," said Lord Greenfield.

"'Tis small enough pleasure," said the duke, and the earl looked at him in some exasperation.

Celeste smiled. "His manners do leave something to be desired," she said. "But I am afraid His Grace is right. My singing leaves nearly as much to be desired as do his manners."

The earl smiled broadly at this. "Well, then, I shall join you," he offered, "and turn the pages for you."

They amused themselves for some time at the pianoforte, with the duke joining in occasionally. They had sung several popular songs when the earl found a piece of music and exclaimed, "Bach! My favorite. Could you play this?" he asked, handing the sheets to Celeste.

She looked at the fugue, with its notes running in all directions, and regretfully shook her head. "It is beyond me," she said.

The earl shrugged. "Never mind," he said. "I find I am tiring of this anyway. Perhaps you would give me a game of chess?"

"Oh, yes," agreed Celeste. Here was something at which she excelled.

"I think it only fair to allow me one final opportunity to try to beat you," said the earl.

"You may try," teased Celeste.

They took their places across from each other at the chessboard, the duke lounging nearby to watch their progress, and before she knew it Celeste had become caught up in the game, all sad thoughts of the morrow forgotten, the fate of her king her only concern.

At last she captured the earl's queen and he grimaced. "I can see that Miss Hart is not one of those young ladies who cater to a man's vanity by allowing him to shine in a game of wits," he complained.

Celeste giggled, then turned thoughtful. After a moment she asked, "Is it not proper for a lady to try to beat a gentleman at something?"

"It is probably not proper for a lady to play chess in the first place," said the duke. "Denotes bluestocking tendancies. But I like a woman who has something in her head besides feathers, and I'll wager Arthur does, too."

The earl nodded. "There is nothing so soothing as a companionable game of chess. I would certainly wish any woman who graced my home to share some of my interests as well as my house."

"Well said," approved the duke. "Which is why Arthur here has been such a tricky fish for those matchmaking mamas to hook. He is looking for a woman who thinks of more than balls and gowns and gossip."

Celeste was only half listening. She was enjoying a pleasant picture of herself and the earl, comfortably ensconced at a chessboard set before a roaring fire while a winter snow quietly fell outside.

Her daydreaming cost her her queen.

The game ended shortly after that, and so did the evening, and Celeste made her way to her bedchamber with leaden feet. *Tomorrow he goes,* she thought. *I wish this castle were enchanted and when the earl made to ride from St. Feylands he'd find himself unable to leave.*

Unfortunately the castle wasn't enchanted. The earl left the following morning, leaving behind the memory of one last brush of his lips on her hand and a smile so full of admiration it had quite made her poor heart give a sick flop.

The duke waved him off and went inside, but Celeste watched his carriage until no more could be seen of it than a trail of dust. Finally she, too, turned with a sigh and went inside.

She spent the morning picking and arranging fresh flowers in vases, an occupation that had pleased her greatly before the earl's visit. But this day she found little pleasure in it. Nor did she find much to please her in the pleasure gardens.

She at last gave up on finding any enjoyment in the day and retired to her bed chamber to write a letter home.

Dearest Mother and Father, she wrote, *I hope this letter finds you both in good health and good spirits. I am well.* That much she could honestly say.

We have had the most splendid houseguest. He is some relation to the duke and is next in line for the title. He is the Earl of Greenfield. Have you heard of him? I found him to be most pleasant. Celeste sighed. I found him to be the most wonderful man I ever met, she thought miserably. Ah, well. If she could not have him for a husband, at least she would have him for a friend. Why did that thought not cheer her?

Celeste abandoned her letter and went to the library, where she spent the afternoon trying to distract her mind from the Earl of Greenfield. That proved a hopeless task, for his smiling face danced on the pages of every book she opened.

She had little appetite for her dinner that night, a fact the duke quickly noticed.

"I suppose you are moping around because you miss Arthur," he observed.

"It was pleasant having some company," said Celeste.

"Pleasant? I should have thought it a good deal more than pleasant having such a handsome fellow about," said the duke in surprise.

"I suppose it would have been pleasant to have even an ogre about," she replied. "For it has been just the two of us rattling around St. Feylands since I came." She laid down her fork and regarded her host. "Do you not occasionally enjoy the company of your fellowman?"

"Occasionally," said the duke. "And only occasionally. My past experiences with my fellowman have taught me that his company most often costs me my gold or else my time, which at my age has become nearly as precious."

Celeste shook her head at him. "You should not be so bitter."

"And you, my dear, should not be so sweet. It is a dangerous thing to be so very trusting of others."

"So you would have me believe," said Celeste.

"So you should know by now," he replied. "Only look at how your family has used you."

"My family has not used me," she said stiffly. "I am here because I wish to be."

"And because neither of your other sisters would come."

"They could not. I am sure you must remember my telling you. I was the only one available."

The duke nodded, his mouth twisted in a cynical grin. "So you said."

Celeste took an angry stab at a potato. "I don't care to discuss my family anymore. They are very good people," she went on. "My mother is the dearest of women, and you'd not find a better man than my father."

"And your sisters are paragons of virtue," added his grace.

Celeste stood. "If Your Grace will excuse me, I find I am no longer hungry. I will await you in the drawing room."

The duke smiled mischievously at her.

He is enjoying this, she thought angrily. The beast!

"Surely you won't want to miss dessert," he said. "It is always your favorite course."

"My appetite is quite ruined," said Celeste haughtily, and flounced from the room.

"We are having Rhenish cream," the duke called after her.

Her step faltered. Rhenish cream. Her favorite. Well, she would just have to miss it. The duke was behaving odiously and she would not countenance such behavior by remaining. She left the room, the duke's barking laugh following her.

He took his time over the rest of dinner, and she was sure he was doing so deliberately to teach her a lesson. Well, it was the duke who needed to learn a lesson, the wicked old man!

He finally joined her, smiling as if nothing was wrong. "Since you are in such an ill humor, perhaps you would like to play chess. Perhaps you will win and finally be able to irritate me, as you have so hoped to do all evening."

Celeste took her place opposite him. Yes, she would very much like to beat him. With a stick. But she settled for the opportunity to outsmart him at chess instead.

The duke trounced her firmly. "Now," he said amiably, "shall we call a truce?"

"I suppose we had best," said Celeste glumly. With a slow smile she added, "Tomorrow night, perhaps, you might enjoy a game of piquet."

The duke smiled at her. "Something in which you think you can beat me, to punish me, so to speak?" Celeste said nothing and he chuckled. "Very well," he said heartily. "Tomorrow you shall have your revenge on me for abusing you so. For tonight, sing me a tune in that flimsy voice of yours. I think we have time for a song or two before the supper tray arrives."

Celeste complied, trying all the while not to remember the earl's pleasant voice singing behind her the night before.

Once again life at St. Feylands fell back into a routine. Celeste involved herself with the running of the castle in the mornings. Early afternoons she spent painting or walking in the pleasure garden or the park. Late afternoons she spent in the library, improving her mind under the duke's tutelage. After dinner they would often have a game of chess or piquet, another game at which Celeste found his grace excelled.

With each passing day, the pleasant idyll that was the Earl of Greenfield's visit became a more distant memory, until, at last, Celeste could almost have believed she'd dreamed the whole thing.

A letter from her mother painfully reminded her she had not. She sat on the stone bench in the pleasure garden and read, *The Earl of Greenfield sounds a most delightful man. Do you think he would do for Dorothea?*

The painful images conjured up by her mother's simple inquiry were more than Celeste could bear, and she fell across the bench and wept.

"Here, now. What is this?" called the familiar gruff voice.

Celeste sat up and hastily wiped her eyes.

She tried to smile, but the duke waved aside her noble gesture. "Don't pretend with me, my girl. I know you are upset. And I can tell you that if your family persists in sending you letters that turn you into a watering pot, I shall forbid them to write."

This outrageous statement brought a tiny smile to Celeste's face. It was sweet of the duke to be concerned about her.

"I know you came out here to enjoy your letter alone," he continued. "And if it had appeared you were doing so, I would have left you in peace." He sat down next to her. "What can that paragon of a mother have said to upset you?"

Celeste could hardly tell the duke her mother's

simple words, or explain her violent reaction to them. She sighed and shrugged. "I am being silly," she said. "I suppose I miss my family more than I ever thought I would."

"Hmmph," commented the duke. He rubbed his chin. "Write your mother and father and summon them to visit us in July. I imagine by then we will be heartily sick of each other's company and will welcome the diversion."

"Oh, Your Grace!" Celeste laid a hand on the duke's arm. "Really?"

"Of course, really. I think it only proper that I should entertain my future in-laws at St. Feylands, don't you?"

Future in-laws. The words fell to the bottom of her heart like a stone and sat heavily there. But, she reminded herself bravely, being wife to the duke would not be so very bad. He was rather sweet, really.

"I suppose I had best invite Greenfield as well," the duke was saying. "Perhaps that older sister of yours may snare him."

Greenfield. There was the reason it would be so bad to be the wife of the duke.

The duke was studying her. "Does that displease you?"

"No, no," she said hastily. "Indeed, it is most kind of you." She smiled at him. "You have been very good to me and my family, and I shall always be grateful."

He patted her hand. "You are a good child," he said. He stood. "I'll leave you to finish your letter in peace."

Celeste watched him go. He was a dear man, undeserving of the cruel trick fate had played on him.

Small wonder he was bitter and a bit cranky at times. Well, his first wife had dissapointed him, but his second wife would not. She would repay the duke's kindness to her family. And it looked very much as if she would pay with a broken heart.

9

THE HART FAMILY was duly summoned to St. Feylands, and at the end of July they came.

"My!" exclaimed Dorothea as she alighted from the carriage. "What a lovely old place. Trust Celeste to land on her feet."

Celeste welcomed her family with open arms, even both her sisters. "I've missed you all so," she said, and hugged her father again.

"Gracious! How would you have had time?" wondered Dorothea. "There must be many wonderful ways to amuse oneself in such a grand house."

"So these are the famous Hart sisters." The gruff voice sounded almost disbelieving.

Dorothea's eyes widened and she stiffened at the sight of the fierce-looking man with the white mane.

Celeste turned and smiled. "Your Grace, please allow me to reacquaint you with my family."

After Celeste had performed the introductions, the duke turned to Mr. Hart. "I imagine the ladies would fancy themselves in need of rest after your journey here. And I imagine you would fancy yourself in need of some masculine company."

"That I would, Your Grace," admitted Mr. Hart with a smile.

"We'll take a turn 'round the grounds, then have a drink in the library. The women won't bother us there, for Celeste knows I'll have no females prowling my library." He led Mr. Hart away, saying, "I have some fine brandy which I am sure you'll appreciate."

"What a rude old man," whispered Emily, when the men were out of earshot.

"Yes, he is," agreed Celeste matter-of-factly. She left the groom of chambers to see to the luggage, reserving for herself the privilege of showing her mother and sisters to their rooms.

The two sisters exchanged looks that at once pitied their sister her fate and showed relief that such misfortune had not come to them as they followed Celeste and their mother off to the guest wing.

Dorothea and Emily's bedchambers were adjoining, and with the Holland covers off the fine old furniture, the rooms were quite impressive.

Dorothea looked into her room in awe. "Why, 'tis twice the size of my room at home," she said.

Emily ran next door to hers and took in the thick carpet, the marble mantelpiece, the massive bed and wardrobe, and sucked in her breath. "Gracious," she managed.

"And Mama, I've saved the best for you and Papa," said Celeste, leading her mother further down the hallway. "Queen Elizabeth herself once slept in your room."

Again, Dorothea and Emily's eyes met, all pity gone

now. Dorothea's glance slid to her little sister, walking down the hallway arm in arm with her mother, and her eyes narrowed.

Celeste, blissfully unaware of the jealousy she had stirred, was watching her mother. Like a young child presenting a bouquet of wildflowers, she waited for her mother's reaction.

Mrs. Hart turned an earnest face to her daughter. "Are you happy here, my poppet?" she asked.

"Mama! What makes you ask such a thing? Have you not seen for yourself what a fine house I live in?" Celeste turned her back on her mother and went to look out the window, afraid that if her mother had a chance to study her face, she could know all. She had never been good at hiding things from that astute woman. "You can almost see the stream from here," she said. "It is just the other side of that copse."

"Celeste, child."

Celeste did not turn around. "The duke has been very kind to me and I am happy here. Who would not be?"

"That sounds like something your sister would say," said Mrs. Hart.

Celeste put on her most sincere smile and ran to hug her mother. "Mama, I am, indeed, happy. Be happy for me."

"I want to be," said her mother earnestly. "Oh, dear child, I want to be." She hugged her daughter tightly.

Celeste made her escape as soon as her mother loosed her hold on her, fearing that if she stayed, that sage woman would see her daughter's eyes were a little too bright, her smile too wide. "Do hurry and freshen up," she called over her shoulder. "I shall have tea waiting in the drawing room."

Once gathered in the drawing room, there was plenty for the Hart ladies to talk about. They caught Celeste up on all that had been happening back home, then proceeded to discuss the plans for Emily's wedding the following June, a subject that made Dorothea purse her lips.

How humiliating, thought Celeste, to be the oldest and the last to find a husband. Her thoughts moved quickly to the Earl of Greenfield, who was expected the following day. Dorothea is greedy for a title and position. She will take one look at my earl and set her cap for him, Celeste concluded miserably. But he's not mine. Nor can he ever be. I am destined to become the Duchess of St. Feylands. He must marry someone someday. So why not let it be Dorothea? Oh, not catty old Dorothea!

"No wonder you volunteered to come to the duke," Dorothea was saying. "I had quite forgotten how splendid St. Feylands is. Look what you will be mistress of. And a title, too."

"Yes, but look what comes with it," pointed out Emily. "The duke is every bit the ogre I remembered."

"Oh, pish posh," said Dorothea, with a flick of her elegant hand. "Look how old he is. He'll be dead within the next five years, most like."

"Dorothea!" Mrs. Hart looked at her daughter in shock.

"Well, 'tis true, Mama," said Dorothea defensively.

"It may be, but I'll thank you to keep a civil tongue in your head. We are guests in the duke's home and he is to marry your sister."

"Lucky girl," said Dorothea. Her smile turned sly. "I'll not envy you your wedding night," she teased.

The Wedding Deception   107

Celeste's face caught fire and Mrs. Hart scolded both of her giggling sisters.

At that moment the rumble of male voices could be heard outside the drawing-room door and Dorothea and Emily stopped their giggling. The door opened, and at the sight of the Duke of St. Feylands Dorothea dropped her smile.

The men joined them and Celeste noticed that her sisters had become extremely reticent in the presence of the duke.

"So," he said, turning his fierce eyes on Dorothea. "You are the oldest, the one who, by right of birth, should have been given the opportunity to come to St. Feylands and try and win the position of Duchess."

Two bright spots of pink appeared on Dorothea's cheeks and she lowered her gaze to her teacup.

Her father came to her rescue. "Actually, we had thought the Earl of Umberland would offer for her. He had, before our family's misfortune, hoped to do so."

The duke grunted. "Umberland needs to marry money," he said. "How very unfortunate for you. You could have had title and position." The blush was spreading across Dorothea's face and Celeste began to think her sister might faint.

But the duke had already lost interest in Dorothea. "And so we come to Emily, the next in line. So you are to wed, are you?"

"Yes, Your Grace," replied Emily in a whisper.

"Speak up, girl! There's no need to squeak like a mouse."

Emily jumped and her mother bridled. "My daughters are unaccustomed to being shouted at, Your Grace," she said.

"Pity," said the duke. "Perhaps they'd have turned

out better if they had been. Don't know how the third one turned out as well as she did," he muttered, and shook his head. He rose. "I pray you will all excuse me. I have some estate work which I had rather not put off. Celeste, you may show your family the castle grounds. That should keep them well occupied until dinner."

With that he left them gaping after him. "Well!" said Mrs. Hart after he'd gone. "I never met with such treatment in all my life. I swear he is worse than the last time we saw him."

Celeste jumped to the duke's defense. "He doesn't mean half he says. Really."

"If he even means half he says, it is too much," replied her mother. She turned to her husband. "John. Let us go home and take Celeste with us. You cannot allow her to marry this monster."

"But he's not a monster," said Celeste. "He really is kind, in his own way." She remembered the hurt the duke had suffered so many years ago. "And besides, he needs me."

"Needs you! Has he no servants to rail at?" retorted Mrs. Hart.

"It is as I said earlier," put in Dorothea. "Celeste has fallen into clover and well she knows it."

The butler was making his stately way to the drawing room with more hot water when he saw the duke bent with his ear to the door and, of all things, stiffling a laugh.

The next day the Earl of Greenfield arrived. The ladies were in the drawing room enjoying their afternoon tea when the butler announced him. In he strode, looking as fresh as if he had just come from the hands of his valet instead of from his traveling coach. His cravat was starched and crisp, his boots gleaming, and not so much as a speck of dust marred his coat. Every glossy black hair was in place.

Dorothea nearly dropped her teacup at the sight of him, but recovered quickly enough to flutter her eyelashes at him when introduced.

Greenfield kissed Celeste's hand, holding it just a little longer than was necessary, she thought with delight. Such an age it had seemed since last he'd held her hand! She lowered her eyes and tried to look composed.

He took a seat next to her and said, "It is a pleasure to meet your family at last. Nearly as great a pleasure as it is to see you again, Miss Hart," he added, smiling at her.

Feeling her sisters must be staring jealously at her, she raised her eyes to his only long enough to give him a shy smile of her own and murmur, "Thank you."

His Lordship turned to Dorothea. "Miss Hart, I believe I saw you in London at the coming-out ball Baron Heshbourne gave for his niece. Alas, we were never introduced."

"Oh, yes," interjected Emily. "I was at that ball also."

The earl nodded. "I remember," he said. "And so busy dancing there was no hope of my securing an introduction."

Emily cocked her head and smiled at the earl, and Celeste, for the first time in her life, learned firsthand what jealousy was. How silly Em looked with that idiotic grin on her face. She was making a complete fool of herself, and if Celeste could have reached her, she'd have kicked her.

"Ah, well," continued the earl. "This introduction to the beautiful Hart sisters is much more satisfactory than a London ballroom, for one has so little opportunity to become acquainted with someone at a ball. But a house party is a different thing altogether." He turned his smile on Celeste. It was more warming than the late July sun and she found herself grinning at him every bit as idiotically as her sister. "Wouldn't you agree, Miss Hart?" he asked softly.

"Oh, yes," she said. "Will you play chess with me again?" she blurted.

"Oh, chess!" scoffed Dorothea. "That is just a stuffy old game for stuffy old men. Besides, only two can play at chess. We shall have to have music and picnics and walks in the pleasure garden." Now she had the earl's attention again, and she obviously intended to keep it. "We found the pleasure garden the most lovely thing imaginable. And that pretty little pond with the goldfish. How delightful!"

Celeste gave up. She sat back in her chair and let the conversation wash over her. Dorothea was determined to have the earl. That was easy to see. Dorothea was beautiful, and an accomplished flirt. She already had the earl eating out of her hand. Well, and who else's hand was there? She was the last Hart girl left. Mama and Papa would be relieved to depart St. Feylands with their last daughter safely engaged. If he offers for her, I shall surely poison her, thought Celeste.

The following day Dorothea launched her campaign to capture the Earl of Greenfield. At breakfast the duke offered to take Mr. Hart about the property. "I imagine you would fancy a ride as well, Arthur," he said to the earl.

"A chance to see St. Feylands' kingdom! That sounds wonderful, indeed," enthused Dorothea.

"Would you ladies care to accompany us?" asked Greenfield.

"I should hate to impose on the gentleman," began Dorothea.

"Very sensible," said the duke, and Dorothea's mouth dropped.

It was one of the few times Celeste had ever seen her sister speechless, and she smiled and poured cream over her porridge.

"We should, of course, be delighted to have the Hart sisters accompany us," said the earl.

Dorothea regained her lost confidence enough to thank him for his invitation and decline on behalf of Emily, who had not yet come down to breakfast. "Emily's a poor housewoman," she said. "She'd most likely fall off her horse before we even got down the drive. And I am sure Celeste is anxious to visit with Mama after having been away for so long."

What would Celeste say? Of course she wanted to spend as much time with her mother as possible. And anything short of declining the earl's invitation would look as if she didn't. She'd been outmaneuvered. She smiled graciously and left the field in defeat.

Emily was not happy when she came down to breakfast and found the earl already gone, and Dorothea with him. "What a selfish creature she is, to be sure."

"My dear, she is only being Dorothea," said Mrs. Hart. "And besides, you already found a man to marry and your sister has not. Let us not begrudge her this opportunity to make a fine match."

"I wish I hadn't accepted Edward," grumbled Emily.

"Celeste is to be a duchess, and Dorothea is going to snag that handsome earl. All I will be is plain old Mrs. Finch."

Her mother smiled at her. "You will never be plain, dearest."

How like Mama to find something kind to say, thought Celeste, and suddenly felt ashamed of her earlier uncharitable thoughts about Dorothea. Mama was right. She must not begrudge Dorothea this chance to get a husband.

That afternoon the earl found Celeste, walking the gravel path to the fish pond. "Did you enjoy your ride, Your Lordship?" she asked.

"Since we are all soon going to be related, don't you think perhaps you had best call me Arthur?" he suggested. "I have already invited your sister to do so."

And invited her to go riding, thought Celeste, and she suddenly found her pleasure in their meeting diminished.

"I feel I have hardly had a chance to say more than two words to you," he continued.

"Of course you said more than two words to me," she replied. "Only last night after dinner you said, 'Your sisters both sing quite well.'" Did she sound jealous? Alas if she did, for she couldn't help it.

"And you said, 'Yes, they do, don't they?' But that was mere polite conversation, and certainly not enough to satisfy a man who had enjoyed so much of your company on his last visit," said Greenfield.

"But my sisters are here this time and I must be a gracious hostess and share," said Celeste, trying to make her voice light.

"Ah, yes," said the earl. "And that you have done

The Wedding Deception   113

very well. It was especially kind of you to allow your sister to ride out with us this morning."

He was watching her. Why? "I neither allow nor disallow Dorothea to do anything," she said. "She is her own mistress."

"I see," said Greenfield, and she wondered if he did. He took her arm, stopping their progress, and at his touch her heart began to thump wildly. "Celeste," he began. "Of course, your sister is very nice—"

They heard a cheery voice calling them and turned to see Dorothea coming down the path. The earl dropped his hand with what Celeste was sure must be a look of regret and smiled politely at Dorothea.

What had he been about to say? Celeste found herself wishing the earth would open up and swallow her sister.

"Such a nice afternoon for a walk," Dorothea said gaily. "Neither too hot nor too cold. Just right. Are you bound for the fish pond, too? I vow it is my favorite spot." She raised a dainty hand to shield her eyes from the sun. "Oh, dear! How foolish of me to come out without my parasol. And you, too, Celeste. We will freckle like mad this time of day. Why don't you run to the house and get mine and we can share."

"Oh, I don't think it is bad," said Celeste, not anxious to be chased off.

"Oh, yes, it is. Mama won't be at all happy if we stay out in this heat without a parasol." She took the earl's arm. "Go on, now. We'll meet you at the fish pond."

Celeste went. There was no sense in fighting over the company of the earl since she was as good as betrothed to the duke, anyway.

She went back to the house and spied Dorothea's

parasol propped outside the French doors of the library. Of course, Dorothea had been outside looking for the earl by herself. She'd seen them going down the walk and conveniently left the thing behind. Celeste shook her head. Perhaps it was as well she was already promised, for she could certainly never compete with anyone as clever as her sister.

She had gotten no more than a few feet when she met Dorothea and the earl coming back up the path. "It would appear we sent you on a fool's errand," said Dorothea with forced gaiety.

"I am afraid it is all my fault," confessed the earl. "I found the afternoon sun especially bright today and the glare was hurting my eyes. Perhaps an hour or two indoors wouldn't hurt." His face lit up with sudden inspiration. "I have it! This would be the perfect time for us to have that game of chess," he said to Celeste. "Dorothea can rest and a little later we can all enjoy a pleasant walk in the garden, after the midday heat has passed."

This time it was Dorothea who had been outmaneuvered. She accepted her defeat with a grace her younger sister found almost unrecognizable and let them go in search of the chessboard.

"Was the sun truly hurting your eyes?" asked Celeste suspiciously as they settled themselves in the drawing room opposite each other.

The earl merely smiled. "Will you go first?" he asked.

With people coming and going, the earl was never able to pick up the threads of their lost conversation, and Celeste didn't know whether to be relieved or disappointed. If he had been about to confess his admiration for her older sister, she was happy he had been cut off, she decided.

But surely he couldn't admire her sister so very much, else he would have gone with her to the fish pond. And surely, if he found Dorothea so fascinating, he wouldn't be looking so admiringly at her.

Oh, what did it matter? she thought crossly as she retired to her room later to dress for dinner. Lord Greenfield can admire me all he wishes, but what good will it do either of us? Even if I were available, it would make no difference, for Dorothea would get him in the end. She has always gotten what she wants.

These thoughts depressed Celeste so very much that she went down to dinner with slow, small steps and an even smaller appetite.

The earl never got around to taking the proposed walk in the pleasure gardens with Dorothea, but she came to dinner undaunted. Celeste was shocked by how very low cut her sister's gown was. And clinging so daringly. Had Dorothea damped it? The earl looked at her admiringly, and Celeste had to admit he'd have to have been blind not to admire the tantalizing sight of her lovely sister in her revealing gown.

The duke eyed her sister with a critical eye, his only comment a disapproving, "Hmmph."

The Duke of St. Feylands still had the power to subdue her sisters, and Celeste noticed that, as on the night before, their dinner conversation was not nearly so sparkling as it was when the family entertained at home.

After dinner the gentlemen joined the ladies and the duke commanded Emily to sing for them. "For it is much better than listening to feminine prattle," he finished.

Emily made her way to the piano, and as she did so the duke shooed Dorothea off after her. "Go and sing something with her, for I am sure you are dying to make a spectacle of yourself," he said.

Dorothea blushed and denied this, saying she was perfectly happy to sit and listen.

"Why don't you sing us a song?" said her father gently.

"Yes, dearest. You and Emily sound so lovely together," added her mother, looking daggers at the duke.

"Sing and be done with it," said the duke. "This conversation wearies me."

Dorothea looked mutinous, but rose, not daring to disobey the duke's command.

But the duke had been right. Dorothea loved to be the center of attention, as did Emily, and once their first song had ended, the two young ladies were delighted to give an encore.

As they searched through the duke's music for something that would please the company, the earl took a seat next to Celeste on the drawing-room sofa. "Your sisters are very accomplished," he said.

The earl must, indeed, be impressed, for hadn't he said the same thing to her the night before? Celeste nodded, wishing she were as accomplished.

"But I'll wager they cannot paint as well as their younger sister," he continued.

Celeste smiled.

The supper cart arrived promptly at ten-thirty, and shortly afterward the duke announced his intention of finding his bed.

Celeste noticed that other than the earl, she was the only one who seemed to give him a truly affectionate good night. It seemed rather a shame, really, that they did not appreciate him more after all he'd done for them. Well, her family didn't know him as she did. In time they would come to love him.

It wasn't long after the duke's departure that Celeste found her eyes feeling scratchy, and the lids heavy. Reluctantly she bid the others good night.

"Let me accompany you upstairs," said Dorothea, and left the room with Celeste as if they were as close as two sisters could be.

Once their candles had been lit and they were out of earshot of both servants and guests, Dorothea's voice lost its sweetness. "A word with you in your bedchamber, if you please," she said, and releasing Celeste's arm, preceded her up the staircase.

Oh, dear, thought Celeste with a sinking heart. She means to berate me for this afternoon.

Sure enough. Dorothea lost no time once the bedroom door was closed behind them. "I do wish you would stop trying to entrap the earl," she said in the scolding, condescending voice Celeste hated. "You are already promised to the duke, so it is very nasty of you to try to put a spoke in my wheel."

"Do you love the earl, then?" demanded Celeste.

"I think he is very handsome. He will do quite nicely," replied her sister.

"But you don't care for him," pointed out Celeste.

"Don't be such a ninny," said Dorothea. "Really, Celeste. I should have thought you'd grown out of such childishness by now. How on earth should I know whether or not I care for him? I have only just met the man. And besides, that has nothing to do with anything, so don't try and change the subject. I'll thank you not to be such a stingy, wicked creature.

Quit trying to capture Greenfield's attention for yourself. You might think of others, you know."

"I have," cried Celeste angrily. "It is what brought me here in the first place. And you might remember that next time you wish to accuse me of being selfish."

Dorothea looked insulted. "What a sharp-tongued thing you have become," she said. "I shall put it down to exhaustion and leave you to get your rest." And with that she swept from the room.

10

Celeste summoned her maid with an angry jerk of the bellpull. How dare Dorothea come to her room and talk to her in such a way? She behaved as though she were a queen and Celeste her lady-in-waiting. Why should her sister's every wish be granted? Why should one and all cater to her every whim? I won't let her have him! thought Celeste. I'll flutter my eyelashes and flirt with my fan and make him mine and that will show Dorothea.

And what good would that do anyone?

The cold voice of reason doused the fires of anger. Celeste sat at her dressing table, staring at the reflection in her looking glass and seeing her future. It was laid out for her and she knew she must leave it unchanged.

And it was small comfort when Smythe shared with her mistress the gossip from belowstairs—the Earl of Greenfield was smitten with one of the lovely Hart sisters, and it wasn't Dorothea. It was the youngest Hart lady everyone said he looked at so admiringly.

Celeste climbed into bed and let the hot tears sting her face. If only, if only . . .

The next morning dawned bright and warm and promised to be a perfect day for a picnic. What could be better, exclaimed Dorothea, than to enjoy an al fresco meal on St. Feylands's grounds?

"And I know just the spot," declared Greenfield. "It is easily reached by carriage, on the banks of the loveliest stream this side of paradise. The grass is greener than emeralds, and willows more graceful than a lady dancing bend their arms over the water."

"Why, how poetic!" exclaimed Emily. She cast His Lordship an admiring glance from under her eyelashes that made her little sister itch to pull her hair. Wicked creature! Engaged to poor Edward Finch and flirting shamelessly with another man.

"Indeed," agreed Dorothea. "I can hardly wait to see such a place. It must be truly inspiring. Or does the Earl of Greenfield always have such a way with words?"

"Oh, no." The earl laughed, shaking his head. "It is simply the magic of the spot." He turned to Celeste. "You will want to bring your sketching pad, for no artist could resist such beauty."

Celeste forced a smile and sent word to Cook to pack a basket.

Two hours later, armed with parasols and a huge hamper filled with every good thing from fresh strawberries to poppyseed cake, the four set out in search of the earl's favorite picnicking spot.

"Oh, my!" declared Emily, when they rounded a

The Wedding Deception

bend in the road and caught sight of the stream. "This is even more pretty than our view at home, and we are on the Thames."

"Didn't I tell you?" teased the earl.

They alighted from the carriage and walked about to enjoy the prospect from various places on the bank while a servant laid out their feast under the shade of a tree.

As they walked Dorothea carried a predominant part in the conversation, but once seated with their meal spread out before them, Emily, who was a lighter eater, managed to monopolize the earl's attention. However, it wasn't long before Dorothea was in control again.

Celeste made one or two feeble attempts to keep up with the verbal maneuvers, and the earl kindly tried to draw her in, but her sisters were determined to keep her out, and neither Celeste nor the earl was a match for them. She gave up at last. Taking up a piece of cheese to nibble and her sketchbook, she propped herself against a tree and began idly to sketch the scene before her.

She became so involved with her thoughts and her sketching that she did not at first hear the earl when he asked to see what she had done.

"Celeste," said Dorothea sharply. "Did you not hear the earl?"

Celeste looked up and found him smiling at her, waiting expectantly.

"I should very much like to see how you have captured paradise on paper," he said.

Gracious! Celeste shut the book and shook her head. "It is nothing interesting," she said. "I was merely amusing myself."

"Then, pray, amuse us all and let us see," implored the earl.

Celeste smiled politely and shook her head.

"Don't be such a ninny," said Emily, snatching up the book.

Celeste tried to grab it back, but Emily was up and dancing away. She turned to the last page and the smile fell from her face. She shut the book and tossed it back down at her sister's feet. "You were right. It is not one of your better works. Let's walk upstream a ways," she suggested.

But the earl was not so easily sidetracked. With a mischievous grin, he scooped up the sketchbook and turned to the offensive page.

Their pastoral surroundings had been quickly sketched in. There was a perfect likeness of himself, and two of his three companions were easily recognized by their dresses. But not their faces, for Celeste had transformed her sisters from the neck up into donkeys.

Dorothea had come to look over his shoulder. She glared at her sister.

The earl was biting his cheek in an unsuccessful effort not to smile.

"That was very wicked," scolded Dorothea, and Celeste found herself blushing, ashamed. "Whatever will the earl think of you?"

"Why, that she is a great tease," said the earl. "And that her sisters must be goodhearted ladies indeed, who can laugh at a prank." He stood and offered his arm to the angry Dorothea. "Shall we walk upstream and explore, ladies?"

Placated, she took it and shot her little sister a triumphant look before taking the earl's arm. Emily was quick to take the other, leaving Celeste to follow behind, banished from the inner circle for her bad behavior.

'Tis no more than I deserve, she thought miserably. That really was childish. Even if it was true. And what must the earl think of me now?

She was given no opportunity to find out, for her sisters continued to monopolize him for the remainder of their picnic and all the way back. Once they returned to the castle, Celeste sought the sanctuary of her room immediately, having decided she had rather not know what the earl thought of her.

But he seemed determined to tell her, for she found him lounging in the hallway outside her door before dinner as if he'd been waiting for her. "May I escort you down to dinner?" he asked.

"I am sure you had rather wait and accompany Dorothea," she replied.

The earl shook his head. "No. I had rather accompany you." He offered her his arm and they started down the hallway. "I had no chance earlier to compliment you on your artistic talent, and I wished to do so. You have quite an eye."

"I am already ashamed enough, Your Lordship. I pray you will not add your censure to my sisters'," replied Celeste, looking away.

"You quite mistake the matter," said Greenfield.

Before he could say more, they were interrupted by Emily, hailing them and waving up from the first landing.

The earl sighed deeply, then smiled and led Celeste down the stairs.

Emily took his other arm and kept up a steady

chatter all the way into the drawing room, where Dorothea was waiting to pounce.

Before she knew it, Celeste found herself separated from the earl with her sisters on either side of him.

"I never before saw such hawklike creatures," commented a gruff voice at her elbow.

She turned and tried to smile at the duke. "They are merely lively," she said.

Dinner was announced and the duke let the subject drop, leading the way into the great dining hall with Celeste on his arm.

Dinner was much as it had been the night before. The duke's presence was still able to daunt even such self-confident young ladies as the Hart sisters.

But once in the more relaxed atmosphere of the drawing room Celeste knew they'd come to life. This would be their opportunity to shine, to show off their musical talent, to angle for seats on each side of the earl, to charm him with conversation and fluttering lashes. And to make sure their little sister got nowhere near him.

Well, it was hardly to be wondered at. With so fine a matrimonial prize as the Earl of Greenfield present, the Hart ladies could hardly be expected to do anything other than vie for his attention.

Their mother, however, found her second daughter's behavior most unexpected. "My dear, you would do well to remember you are engaged to Edward," she chided.

"Oh, Mama. Engagements can be broken," replied Emily, unconcerned.

"Emily!" gasped Mrs. Hart.

"If you break off your engagement, you will get a

reputation as a jilt," said Dorothea, "and then no one will have you, especially not the earl."

"Nonsense," argued Emily. "Who would care if I were to drop someone like Edward. He isn't even an honorable."

"I'll hear no more of this," said Mrs. Hart firmly. "You have made your choice, Emily, and I expect you to stand by it. Edward is a very fine young man and he will make you a good husband. And besides, it is extremely foolish to throw away the bird in the hand for two in the bush."

"Oh, Mother! What do birds have to do with anything?" objected Emily, exasperated.

"Think on it a little," replied Mrs. Hart.

The gentlemen joined the ladies and there was no more talk of birds, or of broken engagements. But, as Celeste had expected, her sisters both came to life, and in spite of her mother's scold, Emily still spent the evening vying with Dorothea for the earl's attention.

During the rest of the week life fell into a pattern. Every day brought forth an activity to please the houseguests. There was riding in the Cotswolds, boating on the stream, croquet on the lawn. And always, there was the fierce competition between the two older Hart sisters for the earl, a competition waged so skillfully it automatically rendered Celeste a bystander.

In spite of the fact that the earl managed just as skillfully to bring her back into the circle every time her sisters shut her out, she felt uncomfortably melancholy.

She watched her sisters playing croquet with Greenfield one late afternoon and wished they'd stayed at home.

The earl knocked his ball into Emily's and she cried

out and slapped him playfully on the arm. "Oh, it is too cruel," she said. "I shall have to go console myself with tea and cakes." She went to where Celeste was sitting under a large oak tree and helped herself to a plate from the table spread with goodies. After filling her plate, she sat down next to her sister. "Well, it is between Dorothea and Greenfield now," she said.

Celeste merely nodded.

Emily studied her. "Celeste, if I didn't know better, I'd swear you were pouting."

"I'm not pouting," insisted Celeste, stung.

"Well, you certainly don't look happy," said Emily. "After all, someone had to be the first to die."

"I know. And I don't care whether or not I am the first one out of the game. I've been left out ever since you and Dorothea came."

Emily looked at her, shocked. "What can this mean?"

"Nothing," said Celeste crossly.

"Why, I believe you are jealous."

"I am not!" cried Celeste.

"You are jealous because of the attention the earl is paying Dorothea and myself," continued Emily, in a voice filled with amazement. "But I don't understand. Why ever should you be jealous of any attention we receive from an earl when you yourself have snagged a duke?"

Celeste looked at her sister. Good heavens! Emily truly didn't understand. It was all a treasure hunt to her. See if you can find the greatest catch.

"Are you really angry with us?" Emily asked.

How could she be angry with her sister when Emily didn't even know she was doing something wrong? thought Celeste. And was it so very wrong? Weren't Dorothea and Emily only doing what they'd been told to do from a very early age—find a suitable husband? But why did finding a suitable husband have to turn sisters into enemies?

Celeste was still pondering this when Dorothea and the earl joined them. "He is too cruel," Dorothea was saying. "It really was most unchivalrous to hit me," she teased the earl.

"Ah, but someone must win," he said.

Yes, thought Celeste. Someone must win. Maybe that is why I am so sad. Because I know that someone won't be me.

She was suddenly very hot, very tired of being outside, very tired of the company of her houseguests. "I think, if you will all excuse me, I shall go inside for a while," she announced.

"Are you not feeling well?" asked the earl in concern.

"I am fine," said Celeste. "It is only that the sun is so very bright. It is giving me the headache," she finished in a choked voice, and hurried away.

The earl made to follow her, but Dorothea laid a restraining hand on his arm, and her words followed Celeste. "She will be fine. Leave her go."

She hurried inside the house, meaning to go straight for her room. But a footman waylaid her with a summons from the duke.

He was waiting for her in the library, standing at the French windows, watching the earl and the Hart sisters make their way across the lawn to the pleasure garden.

"Your Grace?" said Celeste softly.

The duke didn't turn around. "A very pretty picture, that," he said. "Your sisters are now leading Arthur down the garden path." He turned to face her.

"As they've tried to do ever since he arrived. Would you care to come look?"

Celeste shook her head miserably.

"I shouldn't think so," he said. He seated himself at the desk and observed her scornfully. "So this is the family for which you pined."

Celeste hung her head.

"Don't stand there looking like a whipped puppy," snapped the duke irritably. "You cannot help it if you have more honor than both your sisters put together. That's the trouble with being so curst saintlike. Everyone takes advantage of you."

"Only my sisters," said Celeste.

"Yes, yes," he said wearily. "I know your parents are good enough, so there's no need to spring to their defense. Your father's a likable sort, even if he is a fool, and your mother's got spirit, I'll say that for her. Must be where you get it."

Celeste had never thought of herself as having spirit and said so.

"Course you do. Else how could you have managed to come here in the first place? And it takes spirit to stand up to me, I'll grant you, which you did right from the start. It is fitting that the future Duchess of St. Feylands should have spirit. It is also fitting that she should not be made to look a fool; therefore I am ending this farce."

Celeste stared at him, uncomprehending.

"I am sending our houseguests home," he said.

"But you cannot just send them off like so many tradesmen," Celeste blurted.

The duke looked down his hawklike nose at her. "I may do as I please. I am St. Feylands."

"And do you please to humiliate me?" countered Celeste.

"Humiliate you!" roared the duke. "It would seem your own family has done enough of that."

Celeste was blinking, a sure sign of approaching tears.

"Here now," said the duke more kindly. "I have no intention of causing you pain. I should think your sisters have dealt you quite enough this past week. I promise you I shall bring this unfortunate gathering to an end in a most discreet manner. Go on now and have a nap, or whatever it is females do to make themselves feel better."

Celeste went to her bedchamber, curiosity as to what the duke would do temporarily acting as an antidote to her earlier misery.

There was no mention that night at dinner, or in the drawing room afterward, of anyone departing, and Celeste found herself wondering why. Hadn't His Grace said he'd send their houseguests packing? She didn't know whether to be sorry or grateful that he had obviously done nothing, for much as she'd like to see her sisters gone, she hated to part with her parents, and she couldn't imagine how the duke could send them off a week early without hurting feelings.

The following morning Celeste was taking her usual morning turn in the pleasure garden, smelling the flowers, when her father joined her.

"My dear child," he saluted her. "I have just now been speaking with the duke and I must commend you. He tells me he is quite pleased with you and thinks you will make a suitable bride."

Celeste slipped her hand through her father's arm. "What wonderful news," she lied.

"I must say, you seem to have made him very happy," continued Mr. Hart, "for he is much more affable than he was when last we visited him."

"The duke has been very kind to me," said Celeste.

"Indeed, he has," agreed her father. "He has been most generous with our entire family."

Celeste nodded, well aware that the duke's offer to her was a commitment to her family as well. Perhaps he had already offered to help her papa with his financial difficulties. The duke had, indeed, been good to all of them. She should be grateful he was willing to marry such a little nobody as herself.

"Then you will have no objection to marrying him?" asked her father. "I ask you to be truthful, child. For I would rather cut off my right arm than to force you into a marriage you did not wish."

A bargain was a bargain. This was why she'd come to St. Feylands in the first place, as a prospective bride for the duke. Like the princess who found the pea under her many mattresses and so qualified to marry the handsome prince, Celeste had passed the duke's test, whatever it was. And now she was to marry him.

Did she have any objection to doing so? Other than the fact that he was not the Earl of Greenfield, she could think of none. Her father was right. The duke had changed since she'd come to stay with him. He was not nearly so crotchety. And she was fond of him. As the Duchess of St. Feylands she would not have such a bad life. She had the gardens and the library, and perhaps the duke would let her become more involved in the lives of the townspeople. It would be a full and interesting life.

Oh, what did it matter whether she liked the duke or whether she could be happy or anything! She was honor bound to marry him and marry him she would.

"Celeste?"

Her father was waiting for an answer. "I'm sorry, Papa. My mind wandered."

"You were probably thinking of what a fine life you shall have as a duchess," teased Mr. Hart.

Dear papa, thought Celeste. He thinks I am like Dorothea and Emily. Oh, how could he?

She forced a smile. "I shall be happy with the duke. You need have no worries." Even as she said it her throat constricted.

Her father looked at her in concern. "Celeste, child. You do not wish to marry this man?"

"Of course I do," said Celeste determinedly. "And when I do, you and Mama will come stay with us and we shall all be happy as larks."

Here was a vision to hang on to. She would insist her mother and father be allowed to live with them. That would not only make her life at St. Feylands tolerable, it would surely make it most pleasant.

She firmly pushed the image of a handsome, broad-shouldered earl from her mind.

"Very well," said her father. "If you are pleased with the match, then so am I."

There. She had done it!

"The duke suggested we might like to visit London the end of next month and begin preparations for the wedding, as he wishes to be married next spring," continued her father. "As he has also offered us the use of his town house for the duration of the Little Season, he assumed your mother would wish to go home and prepare for her London visit immediately. I think he simply wants his future bride to himself," Mr. Hart teased.

So the duke had managed to find a way to rid them of her sisters. And to seal her fate. "When will I be able to return home?" she asked in a small voice.

Mr. Hart smiled and patted his daughter's hand. "We shall be together for the Christmas holidays. Meanwhile—" Mr. Hart stopped himself. "I forget, I am not to tell you. The duke wishes to surprise you. However, I think I can tell you that what he has planned for you should please you mightily." Celeste was not smiling. "My child, you are pleased, are you not?" said Mr. Hart, and the tone of his voice betrayed both astonishment and worry.

Celeste felt the tears building up. Soon they would refuse to be blinked back and spill out to betray her. "Oh, yes," she said. "Of course I am. Why should I not be? Do go speak to His Grace right away, will you?"

Her heartiness felt so false she was sure her father must see it. He was looking at her, concerned. Anxious to be rid of him, she gave him a playful push. "Hurry, Papa. Before he changes his mind." She dredged up her brightest smile. Her father was still looking at her in concern, but after she gave him one last word of encouragement and another little push, he left her.

She stood a moment, watching him go, the first tears slipping out and sliding down her cheeks, then she ran sobbing down the garden path in the opposite direction.

With her head lowered she didn't see the earl until she'd run into him.

11

"Celeste!" cried the earl, taking her by the arms. "What has happened to upset you?"

"Nothing. It is nothing. Oh, please, let me go," she begged, straining to get away.

"Not until you tell me what has upset you," he said.

"It is nothing I can tell," she cried. "Please release me."

Instead the earl did a very odd thing. He pulled her close to him and put his arms around her, crooning. "There, now. All will be well."

How much she wanted to believe that! For one sweet moment she allowed herself to enjoy the comforting feeling of his strong chest against her cheek. But only for a moment. "You must excuse me," she said, pulling back. "I did not sleep well last night, and I am afraid my nerves are quite overset."

"I think any young lady contemplating marriage to the duke would experience such an overset," said the earl.

"Oh, dear. You know I am to marry the duke?"

"Is that not why he brought you here?" countered Greenfield.

Celeste hung her head and nodded.

"Do you love him?" asked the earl.

Celeste took a step back, insulted. "I am not a fortune hunter, Your Lordship. So you need have no concerns for your relative."

The earl smiled at this. "You certainly are not," he agreed. "A more noble creature I have never met. But you have not answered my question. Do you love him?"

"I am fond of him," said Celeste stoutly.

"Only fond?"

"Many happy marriages have been built on fondness," pointed out Celeste.

The earl nodded. "True," he agreed. He offered her his arm. "Shall we walk?" he suggested.

Celeste looked back at the castle. She should not be out here with the earl. She should leave. Right this minute!

She put her hand on his arm and allowed him to lead her down the gravel path toward the fish pond.

"Are you fond of me?" he asked suddenly.

She felt her face flaming. Oh, if only he knew. "Of course I am," she said.

"More fond than of the duke?"

Celeste looked around in confusion, not sure how to answer. Dissembling did not come easily to her. "I don't know. I suppose not. No!"

He stopped and turned her to face him, and she was conscious of his strong hands on her arms. "If you were free, would you marry me?" he asked.

The Wedding Deception

Celeste's eyes grew wide with fear. "You must not ask such a thing. It is wrong."

"Celeste, I promised I would say nothing, but I must," he began.

"No!" she cried, "Please don't say anything. Don't speak to me, I beg of you. Only let me go!" She broke free from him and ran back up the path, ashamed of her disloyal feelings, ashamed of the fresh tears on her face.

She had no sooner reached the sanctuary of her room than she was summoned to the library. She steeled herself and went downstairs.

The duke and her father were standing together next to a table holding a bottle on a silver salver. Both had a glass of wine. Celebrating, thought Celeste, and felt ashamed that she wasn't happy. How could I be so ungrateful when the duke has been so good to me?

"Your eyes are red," observed His Grace.

"I am afraid I did not sleep well last night," she said, and even as she said it she wondered if she would ever sleep well again. And then, remembering her duty, she added, "I am deeply grateful for the honor Your Grace has bestowed on me."

The duke nodded. "A very pretty speech. I assume your father has informed you of my plans."

Celeste nodded.

"And does a spring wedding meet with your approval?" he asked.

"Yes," she said. She felt she should say something more, but for the life of her she could think of nothing, so she remained where she was, like a servant awaiting orders from her master.

"I am sure Celeste will be very happy," said her father.

"I have been happy with the duke," said Celeste. "I am sure I shall continue to be." There. That sounded very nice. And it was true enough. "If you will both excuse me, I find myself very much in need of rest."

The duke nodded his head and Celeste made good her escape.

She left the library and encountered the earl. "Celeste," he began.

She held up a hand. "Please. You will not say anything to the duke," she begged.

"Don't worry," he said.

"And you must never speak to me again as you did outside," she continued.

"You ask a great deal," said the earl.

"I ask only what is right," she replied.

"I know," he said. "You have a sense of loyalty and a determination to do what is right, no matter what loss to yourself. A man could ask for no better quality in his future wife."

After that speech he bowed to her and entered the library, leaving her to continue on her way.

Instead of going to her room, Celeste went in search of her mother. She found Mrs. Hart in the room adjoining her bedchamber, which had been turned into a sitting room. Mrs. Hart smiled at the sight of her daughter and laid her fancywork aside. "Has your father spoken to you, then, my love?" she asked.

Celeste nodded. "It is all arranged."

"And are you happy?" pressed her mother, searching Celeste's face.

"I believe so," said Celeste. For a moment she felt at a loss, unsure as to how to share her thoughts without worrying her mother. She sat on the footstool and plucked at her gown. "Mama," she said at last, "when you married Papa, did you love him very much?"

Her mother smiled. "Oh, yes. I thought him quite the most dashing thing I'd ever seen." Mrs. Hart stopped her enthusing and looked at her daughter with the same divining look she'd used when catching Celeste at a childhood prank. "The duke is a difficult man," she began.

"Oh, no," said Celeste, springing to his defense. "Not when one knows how to handle him."

"Then what worries you, child? Do you not care for His Grace?"

"I do," said Celeste. "But I certainly don't think he is the most dashing thing I've ever met. I am fond of him though, and I should never wish to hurt him. Is that love?"

"It is enough," said Mrs. Hart. "And it is more than many a bride feels toward her groom. Consider yourself blessed."

Celeste thanked her mother and kissed her cheek. She left the room feeling no better than she had when she'd entered it. Why hadn't she told her mother that although she was fond of the duke, she dreamed about marrying the earl?

She knew why. She had already said it. She would never wish to hurt the duke. And what would become of her family if she didn't stick to the bargain she'd made?

The rest of the day passed in a whirlwind of activity as the Hart family prepared to leave. Dorothea and Emily were both thrilled.

"Whoever would have thought the duke could be so kind as to lend us the use of his town house?" said

Dorothea to Emily, who had come to Dorothea's room to see how her packing progressed.

"Celeste has done us a great service," said Emily. "Just think what our lives would have been had she not wrapped the old curmudgeon 'round her finger."

Dorothea nodded. "And I, for one, intend to take full advantage of our good fortune."

His sister smiled knowingly. "I suppose you shall take the first offer that comes."

"Naturally," said Dorothea, with a self-confident smile. "So Greenfield had better step lively."

"You think he will come to London for the Little Season?"

"Of course he will," said Dorothea. "Along with all the other nobility."

Emily sighed. "I wish I hadn't taken Edward. I could have at least had a baron."

"Ah, well," said Dorothea, unconcerned over her sister's ill luck. "At least you have someone."

"So will you, before the month is out," Emily assured her.

Dinner that night seemed to Celeste to go on forever. She listened to the gay chatter and wondered why they must sit and eat course after course when the first three would have been enough to fill a giant's belly. Would they never be allowed to leave the great table?

But when they were at last all gathered in the drawing room, time seemed to crawl more slowly still. Another song? Oh, must you sing another song? Here is Arthur sitting at my elbow, looking at me in such a way as must make the duke long to call him out, even if they are related. He smells of Hungary water, just like Papa does when he first comes to breakfast in the morning, and I would like nothing better than to have Arthur put his arms around me and—

Celeste firmly reined in her thoughts. It would not do, any more than it would do to remain in this room a minute longer. She feigned a headache and left before the supper tray made its appearance.

The following morning her family was up and on their way early. She stood on the front steps between the duke and Lord Greenfield and waved good-bye, torn between sorrow at losing the company of her parents and relief at seeing the departure of her sisters.

"Now we shall have some peace at last," said the duke. He put an arm around Celeste's shoulders. "Our numbers are happily diminished, and I imagine you and Arthur can find some pleasant way of amusing yourselves this morning while I attend to estate business. We will talk at luncheon. I have a surprise to share with you which I hope will please you."

He smiled down at her, a smile of pure kindness, untainted by either cynicism or mischief, and she remembered the portrait hanging in the gallery. His eyes are smiling, she thought, and the realization warmed her. "I like surprises," she said.

"Good," he said. "Now run along and let me be at my work."

"It is a fine morning for a ride," observed the earl.

A ride! That was what she needed, to ride in the sunshine and laugh, and know that life was good, that she'd at last brought happiness to a man who had been miserable for so long. She ran upstairs to put on her riding habit as the duke made his way to his library.

* * *

In Worcestershire that morning, a beautiful woman with luxurious auburn hair was lounging in her bed, reading her mail. Scattered on the coverlet were various invitations to house parties at some of the most exclusive estates in England. This was hardly to be wondered at. Lady Titania, Countess of Blyss, was at the height of her social power. She had connections everywhere.

As a titled widow with more greed than money, she used those connections to her benefit. Lady Titania was as good at introducing young heiresses into the ton as she was at sending business to dressmakers, and all who benefited from her services rewarded her well.

Ignoring both love letters and the many invitations, Lady Titania picked up the missive from St. Feylands. Their connection was too distant to be recognized, nor had he been to town more than once in the last ten years. Whatever could he want with her? She opened the letter and read:

> My Dear Lady Titania,
> At the end of August I will be sending to you Miss Celeste Hart, a young lady in need of some town bronze. I am counting on you to assist her in acquiring an impressive wardrobe as well as all the right friends. Dropping a hint that this young lady will one day be Duchess of St. Feylands should make your task easy as well as enjoyable.
> Yours, etc.

She chuckled and wondered what squint-eyed little nobody was being foisted on her.

But wait, wasn't there a young lady named Hart presented only last season? A vision of Miss Emily Hart sprang to mind and Lady Titania nodded. A pretty little thing, but a climber. There had been another sister out the year before, she remembered. A conceited creature who liked to put on airs. She'd almost snagged poor Umberland.

Well, so here was another Hart girl. Obviously the Hart family star was on the rise if she'd managed to insinuate herself into St. Feylands's good graces. Surely there must be an interesting tale behind such success.

Her Ladyship tapped her chin with the letter and smiled. How very droll, to be sure.

12

Celeste had second thoughts as she rode down the drive next to the earl. Perhaps she shouldn't have consented to go riding with him. Surely this wasn't proper! Fine time to be thinking of proper, she scolded herself. You didn't think about it when he visited before. She supposed the duke thought himself above the laws of propriety, or perhaps he was unaware of the fact that young ladies should be strictly chaperoned, and not allowed to go riding around the countryside with a young gentleman without so much as a groom to hand. Or perhaps he trusted the earl so very much that he felt such practices to be unnecessary. If only he knew! She found herself wishing heartily that they had a groom trotting along behind to make sure the earl refrained from tempting her.

But the earl spoke no more of his heart, keeping their conversation light and bantering, and by the time they had jumped over a stile and reached open land, she was relaxed and laughing.

"Let's see how good a horsewoman you've become," he said. "I'll race you to the road." And before she could reply, he'd whipped his horse into a gallop.

Laughing, Celeste followed.

Whether her horse had had an extra bag of oats, or whether he simply wanted to catch the horse in front of him, she knew not. She only knew that she was suddenly riding faster than she ever had. Fear gripped her heart as tightly as she held to her sidesaddle. But in spite of her tight grip, she felt herself losing her seat. She tried tightening her knee around the saddle, but it seemed she couldn't get her balance to do so.

Faster and faster the horse went. The wind slapped Celeste's face, stinging her. "Help!" she called, but the cruel wind caught her words and whipped them behind her.

A frightened rabbit bolted in front of her horse and the beast shied, giving gravity the last bit of help it needed to pull her from her seat. With a cry, she fell from the saddle.

At the sound of her cry the earl reined in his horse and turned to see her on the ground. He galloped back, threw himself from the saddle, and knelt next to her. "Celeste!" he cried, and gathered her in his arms.

She blinked up at him. "I am all right," she gasped, but even as she said it she clutched his lapels. "It is just that I was so very frightened." She ended on a sob and he hugged her close.

For a moment she let herself enjoy the comfort of his embrace. But this would never do. It was so highly improper, and, oh, the feelings it was stirring! "Your Lordship," she began.

"Arthur," he corrected.

"We must go back." She felt his breath on her cheek.

His lips hovered longingly near hers. "Immediately," she added.

The urgency in her voice caused him to release her with a sigh. "I'll go fetch your horse," he said. "Can you ride, do you think?"

She bit her lip. "I hate to get back on," she confessed.

He smiled understandingly. "I know," he said. "But it is the best thing you can do."

She nodded and he went to retrieve the horse, which had bolted some ten yards away and was now contentedly pulling up grass. She watched him and knew he couldn't continue to stay at the castle. They would both be miserable if he did.

The earl returned and handed her up onto her horse, and they began their return trip at a sedate pace. "I imagine you will be leaving soon," she said, trying to make her voice sound normal.

Without looking at her, he nodded. "Yes. I suppose I should."

"I think so," she agreed, and they rode the rest of the way back in silence.

That afternoon, as they ate a cold collation, the duke gave Celeste her surprise. She was to go to London for the Little Season, beginning in September, where she would make her social debut.

"Oh, my," was all she could manage.

The duke smiled, well enough pleased with this answer. "Greenfield will escort you, as I have no desire for London frivolities." Celeste's smile faded and the duke's brow fell into an angry "V." "You have some objection to the earl's company?" he asked.

What could she say? "No," she answered slowly, trying not to look at the earl. She felt the warmth of a blush stealing up her neck and hoped the earl didn't look as guilty as she knew she must. "It is only that it might not look very proper."

"You may take your maid, of course," said the duke. "That should make it perfectly proper, as well as the fact you will be traveling in my carriage."

There was nothing more to say except thank you, which Celeste did, trying to sound as enthusiastic as she had felt only a moment before.

But even as she dreaded the temptation of being thrown together with the earl again, she knew she looked forward to seeing him one last time before becoming the duke's wife. God forgive me, she thought. I am a truly disloyal creature.

The earl left the following morning, with both the duke and Celeste to see him off. His good-bye to Celeste was perfectly proper—no smoldering or longing looks. And Celeste found herself both relieved and disappointed.

"There goes the last of our houseguests," said His Grace. "What will you do now that you have no one here to help you occupy your time?"

Celeste set aside her heavy feelings and tried to smile playfully at the duke. "I still have someone here to occupy my time," she reminded him.

"I have work to do. I can't be entertaining you all day," he said gruffly.

"I have work to do also," she said. "And I am going to start it straightaway. I shall go cut some flowers."

He chucked her under the chin. "You are a good girl," he said fondly.

That night at dinner he asked her how she felt about the earl.

"He is very nice," said Celeste.

"Very nice? That is all?"

"He is kind," added Celeste.

"And how do you feel when you hear his name mentioned?" persisted His Grace.

Celeste laid down her spoon. "I don't understand what you mean," she said. "Nor do I understand why you continue to ask me about this man."

"It is because I think, perhaps, you are in love with him," said the duke.

Celeste sat mute, unable to frame a proper answer.

"Do you love me, child?" asked the duke. "A man old enough to be your grandfather?"

Celeste looked at him levelly. "I have become very fond of you."

He nodded slowly, staring at his plate. "I know," he said.

"And I shall make you a good wife," she continued.

"Yes, I believe you would," said the duke. He spoke thoughtfully, as if pondering some philosophical question. "And I think I will make you very happy as well come spring."

Celeste smiled at the duke. The love she bore for him was the love of a daughter to a doting father. Well, surely that was not so bad. As long as they saw nothing of the earl they could be happy. "Do you fancy a game of piquet after dinner?" she asked lightly.

He chuckled. "Yes, I shall allow you to try to beat me. But first you must thank me for the clever way in which I rid the castle of pests."

"Pests?" Celeste looked at him, not understanding.

"Your family," he said.

She smiled reluctantly. "You could certainly have

found no better way to lure them off. Although I shall miss Mama and Papa."

"And they will miss you. But knowing you are well cared for, they'll feel free to enjoy themselves, so don't fret for them. Your father will enjoy his club, and your mother will be happily occupied with planning your wedding. And as for your sisters, they would much rather be in London than here. They will spend these next few weeks happily readying for their visit. Once in London, they will amuse themselves greatly by trying to buy all the right gowns to gain them entrée into society's inner circle come September."

"Gowns," gasped Celeste, suddenly thinking of her own limited wardrobe. "Oh, dear."

"So you do think about such things," teased the duke. "Ah, well. Even the most perfect of females, it would seem, must have her little flaws. Never fear. You shall have gowns. Lady Titania will see to that. And you shall wear those gowns to houses your sisters will only see in their fondest dreams."

The rest of the summer passed without event, and Celeste and the duke fell into a pleasant routine. She entertained herself during the day, spending her mornings seeing to the running of the castle or diligently stitching an altar cloth for the church. Afternoons, she read or found a pleasant spot outside to sketch.

The servants already acknowledged her as their mistress and were all fond of her. Mrs. Griffon especially took an interest in her and guided her as she learned the duties of a lady of a great house.

In the evenings she and the duke played chess or piquet, or discussed whatever book she happened to be reading. Sometimes she'd play the pianoforte and sing for him, although he still considered her singing less than pleasing and was quick to say so.

The duke's gruff comments no longer bothered her. She usually ignored them. Sometimes she'd offer a clever retort and he'd chuckle and tell her she had spirit.

That I do, she thought one day. Maybe that is why I have been able to survive so fierce a trial. At any rate it is no longer such a trial, so either the duke has become kinder or I have grown fiercer.

"Shall I do well in London?" she asked him one night.

"You are beautiful and my name will clear a path before you in society. Of course you will do well," replied the duke.

"No, I mean my manners."

"What the devil is wrong with your manners?" demanded His Grace.

"Nothing, I hope," said Celeste. "It is just that I seem to have changed since first I came to the castle. I am not quite so—" She stopped, searching for a word.

"Sweet?" supplied the duke.

She blushed. "I have become used to dealing with you," she said.

The duke threw back his head and laughed. "And a good training it has been for you. You shall do famously in London, I assure you."

But as the day of her departure grew nearer, Celeste found herself becoming increasingly nervous. Was it simply jitters over her London debut, or the realization that soon the Earl of Greenfield would arrive to escort her there?

By the day of His Lordship's expected arrival she was in a state, indeed. Her trunks had been packed and unpacked several times, and there was now nothing more she could do to ready herself for her trip. She had gone over the meals for the next three months, planning everything from the soup course to dessert, to be sure the duke would have his favorite dishes often. But all her labors left her restless rather than rested. "Mrs. Griffon, we should put out fresh flowers," she fretted.

"But Miss Hart, we put fresh flowers in the vases only yesterday."

"They look droopy," insisted Celeste.

Mrs. Griffon gave up and agreed with her mistress that on closer inspection, the flowers did, indeed, look a little wilted.

They had just finished their task when the Earl of Greenfield arrived. He came upon Celeste putting a vase in the drawing room.

"Such industry!" he observed. "Might I hope it is on my behalf?"

Celeste turned, and her rebellious heart leaped as if trying to get at him. Her feet were no better behaved, for they carried her to him, arms outstretched. "Your Lordship! How good to see you."

He caught both her hands in his. "Let me look at you, then. Can it be possible? You are even more beautiful than the last time I saw you. Life with the old curmudgeon must agree with you."

Before Celeste could answer, the old curmudgeon himself came through the door. "Poisoning the girl's mind against me, Arthur?"

Unabashed, the Earl of Greenfield heartily greeted the duke and told him he looked in fine fettle. "Life with a lovely young lady obviously agrees with you."

"Life with this particular young lady agrees with

The Wedding Deception   151

me," corrected His Grace. "Most young women have more hair than wit. Celeste is an exception. She entertains herself and is not always pestering me to take her here and take her there."

"And how have you been entertaining yourself?" asked the earl as they seated themselves.

"I have stitched an altar cloth for the church, and every Saturday I go there to arrange the flowers for Sunday. And, of course, I have my entertainments here."

"Such as?" prompted His Lordship.

"Oh, I assist Mrs. Griffon," said Celeste airily. "And I still have all those books in the library to get through. Then there is my drawing." Mention of her drawing brought to mind a certain picnic earlier in the summer and Celeste colored.

The earl merely smiled and said he was glad she hadn't been bored in the duke's company.

"My company is considerably more interesting than the company of any of the feather-headed females she'll meet in London," said His Grace.

Celeste was sure she would enjoy London very much, but refrained from saying so. Three months to enjoy the company of the earl! How she had looked forward to it, even though she'd tried not to.

In spite of the fact she had looked forward to seeing the Earl of Greenfield one last time, Celeste found herself nervous about spending so much time with him in a closed carriage. She found her heart fluttering as he handed her up the following morning and climbed in after her. Surely the duke must be either blind or a fool to let them go off together like this, she thought miserably. Smythe might be along to lend propriety, but her presence could hardly keep them from falling even further in love.

Once seated, she let down the window and looked at the duke. Couldn't he see the effect the earl had on her? Surely it must be written all over her face. Her benefactor was smiling benignly on her. He had been so good to her. She felt every inch the traitor looking at that smiling face, and tears pooled in her eyes.

"Here now," said His Grace gruffly. "I'll not have you turning into a watering pot when you are about to set out on such a great adventure."

"I shouldn't leave you," she said.

"Nonsense. You must have your season. Can't have a nobody for a duchess." He reached up and took her hand. "I shall miss you, child," he said. "Give a thought once or twice to your old curmudgeon."

He squeezed her hand and stepped back from the carriage.

The steps were let up, the whip was cracked, and the horses sprang forward, pulling Celeste away from the castle and toward the city of pleasure and temptation.

THE TEST OF LOVE

13

As a child, Celeste had always loved London, but as a young lady making her social debut she found it an even more wonderful place. Lady Titania had taken to her the moment she met her, declaring Celeste the most beautiful creature she'd ever seen and taking her out the day after her arrival to every shop in Leicester Square and Oxford Street. Dressmakers were commissioned to make her the kind of wardrobe her sisters had only dreamed of, and Celeste was amazed to find how many different dresses a lady of fashion required.

"This is going to cost the duke so very much," she said to Lady Titania. "Are you sure I must have dresses even for riding in a carriage?"

Lady Titania chuckled. "Yes, my dear. I am sure. And don't worry about cost. The duke can well afford it. He has instructed me to make sure that as a future duchess you are properly attired, and I intend to do just that."

Celeste said no more to Her Ladyship. But she did

worry. Dresses, fans, slippers, half boots, silk hose, bonnets. Oh, dear!

If only Lord Greenfield would call. She could ask him about all this wanton spending. Alas, she had seen little of the earl since the day he had escorted her to Lady Titania's. He had said he wouldn't be long in town, as he had estate business to attend to, but she had felt sure he would at least remain to see her through her first ball.

She was sure it was nothing more than noble sacrifice that kept him from spending time with her, and she found herself vacillating between relief and misery (at least as much misery as a young lady with a new wardrobe and her first ball to look forward to could experience).

The day Lady Titania took her to the Exeter Change to purchase several fans Celeste nearly rebelled.

Lady Titania scowled at the painted silk fan she had unfurled and shut it with a snap. "My dear child," she said. "A fan is a most necessary tool."

"Can I simply not purchase *one*?" asked Celeste in a small voice.

Lady Titania eyed her charge. "Are you worrying about spending the duke's money again?" she accused.

Celeste blushed, but was spared from answering by the approach of a handsome young man with fashionably cut fair hair and broad shoulders. "Just as I thought," he said. "It is, indeed, Her Ladyship."

Lady Titania was suddenly all smiles. "Lord Cheshire! Just the man I need at such a difficult moment."

"Difficulties? How may I smooth them away? Slay a dragon? Fight off brigands? I am at your service for any great deed save filling my carriage with your parcels. Sadly, my mother has already managed to fill it to overflowing."

Her Ladyship smiled coquettishly. "No, sir. No such service is required. In fact, I must ask of you a task infinitely more difficult. I pray you would help me convince my young friend of the necessity of owning more than one fan. Lord Cheshire, allow me to introduce to you Miss Hart, who is new to us this season."

Lord Cheshire had already been casting a frankly admiring look at Celeste. Now he swept her a bow and took her hand reverently. "Miss Hart? I should have thought your name to be Aphrodite."

Thanks to the duke's fine library, Celeste knew exactly who Aphrodite was and she blushed and lowered her eyes. "You are too kind, Your Lordship," she murmured.

"No, not nearly kind enough," he corrected.

"Miss Hart feels that one fan should suffice her for the season," put in Her Ladyship.

Lord Cheshire looked shocked. "One fan only? Impossible. How can a lady attend a card party, the theater, go driving, or even attend church with only one fan? As much as you will need to use yours, it would be very much worn out before the week was out."

"There, now," said Lady Titania firmly. "That settles it." She turned to His Lordship. "You have been of great service, sir."

"Then will you reward me by allowing me to solicit Miss Hart's hand for a dance at Welthams' ball next week?"

Lady Titania inclined her head. "I will." She looked mischievously at Celeste. "If the lady herself agrees."

Lord Cheshire seemed a very nice young man. And Celeste thought it would be nice to know she'd have someone to dance with at her first ball.

"I should be happy to dance with you, Your Lordship," she said gratefully. "Thank you so much for asking me."

The young earl's eyebrows shot up. "Aphrodite thanks me?" He broke into a broad smile. "No, it is I who must thank you, and count myself fortunate for meeting you today and getting a jump on all those other jackanapes who will swarm around you once they hear of your arrival in our city. Now I had best return to my mother, who most like has need of me."

"What a nice man," said Celeste after he'd left them. "And so good to his mama."

"He should be," said Her Ladyship. "His mama has a great fortune, which will be his one day if he does nothing to anger her."

Celeste's brows knit. What had Lady Titania meant? "Surely His Lordship isn't nice to his mother simply because she is rich," she said.

"It certainly isn't because she is kind," said Her Ladyship. "The old woman is a dragon."

Celeste had little time to ponder Her Ladyship's odd remark. She was dragged ruthlessly on to another stall, where she was presented with more fripperies on which to squander the duke's money.

The following day the ladies paid morning calls, Lady Titania presenting Celeste to the various society notables and patronesses of Almack's. Before the morning was out, they had procured the necessary vouchers to provide Celeste an entry into those select rooms. "Now you are assured social success," said

Her Ladyship. "For without those vouchers you would have no hope of entering the ton."

"I remember how hard my mama worked to get vouchers for Dorothea and Emily," said Celeste. "It must be a very grand place, indeed."

"It is anything but," said Her Ladyship. "The dance floor is poor, the refreshments deplorable, and the company often stuffy."

"Then why go?" wondered Celeste.

"To be seen, of course," said Her Ladyship with a tolerant laugh.

And Celeste was seen. With her perfect features and figure, dressed in an expensive gown, and in the company of Lady Titania, she could hardly have been missed. She was immediately surrounded by admirers and, before the evening was over, she had more requests for dances at the ball than she would have to give. "And that nice man Mr. Brummell even asked me to dance," she told Her Ladyship as they drove home.

"Ah, so that is what he was asking you. That wretched Lady White was bending my ear and I couldn't hear a thing he said. Well, you are bound to be a success if you dance with the Beau."

"Oh, dear," said Celeste.

"What is it?"

"I am afraid I told him I didn't think I would be able to dance with him, because so many other men had already asked for dances."

"What?" Her Ladyship was incredulous. Then a slow smile grew on her face. Finally she threw back her head and laughed uproariously.

"What is so funny? I don't understand," said Celeste.

"Oh, it is too rich. The Beau himself turned down.

You will be the talk of the town by tomorrow," predicted Her Ladyship, wiping her eyes.

And so she was. *But I fear it is costing you a great deal of money to keep me here,* she wrote the duke. *Thank goodness Her Ladyship said I need not worry about being presented until spring, as this is only the Little Season. Such a name for something which seems to be so big and grand! Do you not find that strange? At any rate I am glad enough to escape being presented, for I hear Court gowns are terribly expensive. I would have you know that I have tried to keep costs down. . . .* Celeste sighed. She hoped the duke wouldn't be too very angry with her over all this mad spending. She bit her lip and continued to write, *and I have vowed to have no more gowns made for me, no matter what Lady Titania says. I already have twice the number of gowns Emily had last spring for her debut.*

Celeste stopped her writing. She wondered why she had seen nothing of her sisters and mother. Surely she should have met them when she and Lady Titania were paying calls. Well, she would make sure she called on them before the ball.

Later that day Celeste timidly mentioned that she would like to pay a call on her family, and Lady Titania assured her they would do so as soon as time permitted.

But time did not permit, for Lady Titania kept Celeste so busy it seemed she barely had time to breathe, let alone go to see her family. Every day was packed with shopping, social calls, even lessons with a dancing master, to make sure Celeste would not disgrace herself at the ball. "Now that you have permission to waltz we must make sure you can do so, and do it well," said Her Ladyship.

Celeste made no objection to Lady Titania's plans for her, but she did wonder when she would ever get an opportunity to call on her family.

Before she knew it, the day of the Welthams' ball had arrived and Smythe was doing her hair. "Perhaps I shall see Mama and Em and Dorothea at the ball," she said. "What do you think, Smythe?"

"I should think so, Miss Hart," said Smythe. "And I should guess their eyes will fair pop out when they see you." Smythe looked lovingly at the ice-blue satin gown. "Such rich material, and so finely made. You are bound to be the envy of every woman there."

She clasped the necklace of pearls, which had arrived for her from the duke only that day, around Celeste's neck and Celeste studied herself in the looking glass. With her hair done up, her new necklace, and her low-cut expensive gown she felt very grown up, indeed. Well, and so she was! She was now officially out and engaged to be married, and she was wearing a gown her mama would never have allowed her to wear only a year ago. And if that didn't mean she was grown up, then she didn't know what did. She smiled at her reflection, well pleased. "I do hope Lord Greenfield will be at the ball," she said.

Smythe smiled sympathetically and said she hoped so, too, and as her mistress left the room she said to herself, "Poor thing."

The ballroom in the Welthams' expensive town house made Celeste think of the pleasure gardens back at the castle. The scent of roses sweetened the air, and the rainbow colors of the ladies' fine gowns reminded her of the garden blooms she'd so happily sketched a few months back.

She wondered how the duke was amusing himself back home. Was he thinking about her? She fingered her pearls and remembered the kind note accompanying them. *I have no doubt you will be a success*, the duke had written. She hoped so. She would hate to disgrace him.

She searched the room for the Earl of Greenfield but didn't see him, and this failure stole a little of the warm glow from her heart.

"Here you are," said Lord Cheshire, smiling at her. "I believe my name is the first on your dance card."

Celeste recalled her wandering thoughts and smiled at His Lordship and let him lead her onto the floor. It would have been so nice to have the duke here to see her at her first ball. And it would have been even nicer to have the earl present, comforting even, for as she walked out onto the floor she discovered that a ball can be a rather frightening thing to a young lady newly grown up. She swallowed hard and bowed to her partner. Well, there is no turning back now, she told herself firmly, then pushed away the uncomfortable thought that this applied to her upcoming nuptials as well.

There was little time to think once the dancing began. And before long Celeste was enjoying herself very much. Indeed, it would have been hard to do otherwise, she realized, with so much twirling and hopping and laughing, and kind young men fetching her punch and going out of their way to amuse her. Lord Cheshire took her in to supper and proceeded to tell her that no other woman in the room could hold a candle to her, turning her face pink with pleasure.

Her biggest thrill came when Lord Greenfield walked into view and announced he had come to claim her for a dance. "Oh, how wonderful!" she declared. "I had not seen you at all, and thought perhaps you had already gone back to your estate."

"I wished to stay and see you a social success," he said. "And I can see you are."

Celeste lowered her eyes demurely. "I am having a very good time," she said. "But I still don't know how to properly use my fan."

He chuckled. "I am sure you will learn. The music is starting. Shall we?" He held out his arm.

She made to go with him but checked herself. "Oh, dear. Are you sure I have this dance with you? My dance card is filled and—"

The earl held up his hand. "Say no more. It was filled, but I was able to persuade one of your partners into giving up his dance with you."

"You were?"

The earl nodded. "He owed me a considerable sum of money. I forgave his debt." Celeste's eyes widened and the earl smiled. "Come, let us dance."

Other dancers were beginning to swirl about the room. "A waltz!" exclaimed Celeste.

The earl nodded. "I know," he said with a smile.

Never had a dance been so intoxicating. The earl's hand on her waist produced a pleasant warmth and made her heart flutter like an excited bird. He was smiling at her, a loving, possessive smile, the kind of smile a man gave to the woman he loved, and she felt she would burst with happiness.

A shadow moved over her heart as she realized this would not do. Lord Greenfield had no right to smile at her in such a way, and she should not be encouraging him. "Perhaps we should sit down," she suggested. "I find I am suddenly very warm."

"Very well," he said, still smiling. He escorted her to a gilt chair, then went in search of punch.

Sadly she watched him go. I should run away and not be here when he returns, she thought.

"Miss Hart," said a voice at her elbow. "Are you not feeling quite the thing?"

It was Lord Cheshire, smiling so kindly, and looking at her in such concern. "I am afraid I was suddenly very warm," she said.

"Here, then. Let's go out on the balcony. A breath of fresh air is what you need."

Oh, yes! Here was her chance to run away. The earl would come back and find her gone. Then he would go away, go home and leave her alone. The thought of not seeing the earl anymore was almost enough to keep her in her chair, but her sense of honor pulled her up. "That would be nice," she said, taking Lord Cheshire's arm.

"There," he said, once out of the ballroom. "Is that not better?"

Celeste could hear the music waltzing out to them from the ballroom. Even now Lord Greenfield must be looking for her. It was rather chilly out. She could feel the goose bumps rising on her skin. Perhaps this hadn't been such a good idea. She shivered.

"Oh, now you are cold," said Lord Cheshire sorrowfully. He took off his coat and draped it over her shoulders. But instead of removing his hands from her arms, he left them there. "Is that better?" he asked.

Oh, dear. This *surely* wasn't proper! What if someone were to find her here like this with the Earl of Cheshire? She'd be compromised. What would the duke say? What would Lord Greenfield say? He would think her a fast, fickle thing, indeed.

"You are the loveliest creature I have ever seen," Lord Cheshire murmured.

Celeste felt his breath close to her ear. Gracious! With a wildly pumping heart she squirmed out of his grasp and his coat fell to the ground. "I think I had best go in," she said, and bolted for the balcony door. She threw it open only to find a broad chest blocking her exit.

14

Celeste let out a startled yelp and looked up into the eyes of the Earl of Greenfield. "Oh, thank goodness," she breathed.

"Your punch," he said, holding up the crystal cup. "Come, let's find a seat."

Once again the earl led Celeste to a chair, and she sank gratefully onto it, finding her knees suddenly very weak.

"If the duke were here, he would possibly misinterpret your actions," said Greenfield gently.

Celeste hung her head. "I was very foolish," she said.

"I know," he agreed, and the smile in his voice took the sting from his words. "You must be careful, Celeste. People will talk if you let men get you off alone. They will say you are fast. I cannot stay here and watch over you, for I promised the duke I'd not meddle with your come-out, and I must, in good conscience, keep my word to him."

So that was the real reason Lord Greenfield was going to make himself scarce. A cloak of misery settled over Celeste, making her shoulders droop. Why hadn't the earl said he couldn't stay because he was in love with her and she was promised to the duke? What kind of silly promise was this? She didn't want him to go. A tear danced at the corner of her eye.

"Now, don't cry, dear one. You are supposed to be having fun tonight. What will people think if they see you sitting with a sad face, but that I am the greatest of brutes?"

"You are!" cried Celeste. She jumped out of her chair and ran away from him, leaving him looking wistfully after her.

Celeste found Lady Titania flirting with a rotund gentleman with wispy gray hair. "Celeste, dear child," began Her Ladyship.

"I wish to go home," said Celeste.

"What?" Lady Titania looked stupefied. "Are you not having a good time?"

"No," said Celeste frankly.

Now Her Ladyship looked horrified. "Oh, you poor girl. It must be a megrim coming on." Her Ladyship turned to her companion. "She had one only the other day. You must excuse us, Your Grace. I shall have to present Miss Hart when she is feeling more herself."

Lady Titania bustled them away from the portly gentleman, steered them through a river of admirers and into the powder room. "Now, what is this all about?" she demanded crossly.

Her sponsor's anger brought the tears out of hiding and they raced down Celeste's cheeks. "Please," she said, grabbing at the excuse Her Ladyship had offered earlier, "I don't feel at all well. May we go home?"

"Well, that is more the thing," said Her Ladyship, somewhat mollified. "Remember, you must never say you are not having a good time. A headache is always acceptable. But never boredom. It is the highest possible insult to your hostess."

Now thoroughly miserable, Celeste found her handkerchief and buried her face in it. Her first ball, and she had made a miserable botch of things. Whatever would the duke say?

"There, now," said Lady Titania, patting her arm. "It is not the end of the world. Things will go better next time."

Lord Greenfield was leaving London. Celeste was sure things would never go better again, and once safely inside Lady Titania's carriage, she indulged herself in a good cry.

Lady Titania said nothing, but sat looking thoughtfully at Celeste as they made their way through the quiet streets of Mayfair.

Although she had her moments of melancholy, Celeste found it impossible to be miserable all the time, even though she felt she should be. But there were so many new and exciting things to do: routs, balls, loo parties, drives in Hyde Park. "And look at these presents!" exclaimed Lady Titania one day. "You have received enough sweets to start a confectioners shop."

It was true. There wasn't a day that she didn't receive some token from an admirer, especially from Lord Cheshire, who had sent her flowers and a box of sweets from Gunther's the day after the fateful ball, with a note of abject apology.

"You are a success," proclaimed Her Ladyship. "I am sure the duke will be proud."

"So will Mama," added Celeste. "May we go call on my family today?" she asked.

Lady Titania had her orders. "My dear, it would be delightful to call on your family and meet your dear mama and sisters, but I am afraid we are at home today. It would never do to have callers come and find us gone."

"Perhaps I might go alone?" suggested Celeste.

Lady Titania shook her head. "Most of our callers will be coming to see you, silly child." She patted Celeste's hand. "Perhaps tomorrow," she said.

Celeste nodded, disappointed. She suspected that when tomorrow came there would be some other pressing social obligation that would prevent her from seeing her family.

And it was as she expected. The following day Her Ladyship had more plans for Celeste that couldn't be altered. But in spite of Her Ladyship's careful plans, the morrow did bring a family reunion. That evening at Almack's someone tapped on Celeste's shoulder. She turned to see her sister Emily. "Emily!" she cried happily, and hugged her.

Emily submitted stiffly to Celeste's embrace. "I am surprised you deign to recognize me now you are such a grand lady," she said.

Celeste drew back and stared at her sister. "What can you mean?"

"You know very well what I mean," snapped Emily. "Never calling, never being at home to us when we sent up our card."

"I never knew you called," protested Celeste.

Emily made an impatient face. "I just thought you

The Wedding Deception

should know that Mama is heartbroken from your neglect. Other than that, we fare fine enough, considering we are unable to move in the same exalted circles as our little sister."

Celeste knew not what to say. "Oh, Emily," she began.

At that moment Lady Titania came upon them. "Celeste, dear child. The Duke of Chinchester has been waiting to talk with you this age." She took Celeste's arm to lead her away.

"Lady Titania! Look who I have found," said Celeste eagerly. "It is my sister Emily. Emily, allow me to present you to Lady Titania."

Her Ladyship nodded coolly and told Emily it was nice to meet her. "I hope you will excuse us," she said, and gave Celeste's arm a tug, forcing her to come away.

"Oh, dear. Now she will be angry," said Celeste.

"That may well be," said Her Ladyship, unperturbed, "but she will recover."

"But why did we have to leave?" protested Celeste. "This is the first I've seen of any of my family, and they think I am neglecting them."

Lady Titania gave Celeste a stern look. "And for good reason. Association with your sisters can do you no good, and it is the duke's wish you spend as little time as possible with them."

So that was why Lady Titania had never found the time to pay a call! Celeste's face took on a mutinous look. "Nevertheless they are my family," she said.

Her Ladyship sighed. "Then you may pay them a call tomorrow," she said wearily. "But I can promise you the duke will not like it."

"He will simply have to be displeased, then," said Celeste firmly. "For I cannot neglect my family."

They were joined by another lady and the conversation was ended, but Celeste continued to replay it in her mind.

And she continued to do so, long after they had returned home and she had been readied for bed. "I shall write the duke first thing in the morning," she announced to the empty room, "and tell him I intend to see my mother and sisters. After all, right is right."

The following morning as she sat in the drawing room of the duke's town house, she wondered why she had wished to do right. Her father was out, so she was denied the pleasure of seeing him. And while her mother was glad to see her, that woman's pleasure in her company couldn't offset her sisters' bitterness.

"I wonder you had time even to pay a morning call," said Dorothea.

"Yes," put in Emily. "Now that you are such a grand lady with such grand connections you have no time for your own family."

"It has been most unkind of you to neglect us so," continued Dorothea. "If I were in your slippers, I would be using my connections to help a sister, I assure you."

"And so I shall for you," said Celeste earnestly. "Really, I had no idea you had called at Lady Titania's. In fact, I had been wondering why I had heard nothing."

"Well, it is water under the bridge now," said Mrs. Hart. "And we are all very glad to see you."

"Yes," agreed Emily. "My, but that is a fine walking gown," she added, looking at her sister's dress with a greedy eye.

"I suppose the duke has given you any number of new gowns," said Dorothea bitterly.

"Yes, he has. But didn't he do the same for both of you?"

Dorothea shrugged and Mrs. Hart answered. "The duke has been very generous. Naturally we didn't like to take too great advantage of such generosity."

"Naturally," murmured Celeste, and wondered how soon she could politely escape. Perhaps the duke had been right about not spending time with her family.

She stayed to drink a cup of tea, then made her excuses and rose to leave.

"Before you leave, dearest, I would have a word alone with you," said her mother, and dismissed her sisters.

They each hugged their little sister and left, seeming happy enough to go since their grievances had been aired.

Celeste sat back down on the sofa, wondering what her mother could possibly have to say to her that demanded privacy. Was Mama angry with her for neglecting them?

"Your father and I are both very proud of you, my poppet," said Mrs. Hart.

"Thank you, Mama," said Celeste. Surely this wasn't why her mother wanted to speak with her alone, simply to tell her she was proud of her.

"I know you are very busy these days," continued Mrs. Hart. "Please don't feel you need to take us up."

"But Mama, I want to be with you," Celeste protested.

Her mother smiled and patted her hand. "And so you will be. After you are married I am sure the duke will allow us to visit you. But for the time being I think it best we see little of you."

"I don't understand," said Celeste.

"You are moving in exalted circles these days. Your family can do you no good. We are gentry, child, not nobility."

"But Dorothea and Emily," began Celeste.

Mrs. Hart was shaking her head. "Are both very selfish. You have sacrificed enough for them already. You owe them no more. Take your good fortune and enjoy it, for of all my daughters you deserve it the most."

"Oh, but Mama," began Celeste. "Don't you want Dorothea to make a good match? There is much I can do for her."

"And much she can do to you," said Mrs. Hart. "My dear, you must allow me to know what is best. Dorothea had her chance. She could have gone to the duke and she chose not to."

"But that was only because she was sure the Earl of Umberland would offer for her," said Celeste, defending her sister.

"She had other offers. She held out for Umberland. It was a gamble, and she lost. But never worry. Your sister will land on her feet. If she is still unattached after you are married, then you may help her." Mrs. Hart rose, concluding the interview before her daughter could protest further.

Celeste left her mother with a heavy heart. Surely Mama couldn't be so in awe of her new position that she felt intimidated by it. Had the duke, perhaps, made her mother feel their presence in her life would be unwelcome?

I have had a most unpleasant shock, she wrote the

duke. *My sisters believe I have purposely had nothing to do with them while they are in town. My mother feels the family does not belong in the circles in which I am moving. Who could have put such an idea in her head?*

The duke's reply was swift and short. *Wonder no more who put such an idea in your mother's head. It was I. Your sisters are scheming harpies who do not deserve to share in your triumph. They have already received more than they deserve from my hand, and should be thankful for their new gowns and the use of my town house. Your memory is short. Mine is long. Say no more to me on the subject.*

Celeste laid aside the letter. Such a hard man! Where was kindness? Where was mercy?

Lady Titania entered the sitting room. "Ah, I see you, too, have had a letter from the duke."

Celeste looked sadly at Her Ladyship. "He is a hard man," she said.

"Life has hardened him," said Lady Titania. "But he is also fair. And he has been more than fair with your family. Your parents are wise enough to know it."

Celeste dropped the subject. It would do no good to badger His Grace, or Lady Titania, either, who did the duke's bidding. Perhaps the duke would reconsider and at least allow her to invite her family to Lady Titania's ball in November.

The days hurried past in a swirl of activity, turning into weeks. Admirers continued to flock to Celeste's side, in spite of the fact that she had let it be known she was betrothed. "Why do these men continue to send me gifts," she asked Lady Titania, "when they know I am already engaged to be married?"

Her Ladyship smiled at Celeste and shook her head. "Silly child. They all hope to win your favors. You are marrying a man much older than yourself. It is assumed you will take a lover."

Celeste's face turned pink. The image of Lord Greenfield tiptoed into her mind and her color deepened. "I would never do such a thing," she said stoutly, to herself as much as her mentor.

Lady Titania studied her. "I believe you wouldn't," she said. "Foolish, noble child. However did St. Feylands find such a treasure?"

Celeste felt the heat on her face increase. She knew how very disloyal she was. The poor duke. Was she doing him any service at all in marrying him? What if she turned out to be like his first wife, loving fun and parties more than her husband and home? She certainly had been enjoying herself. And could she trust herself not to run off with another man and break the poor duke's heart all over again? Celeste set her jaw. She wouldn't hurt the duke. Having made such a resolve, she went to her room to write him a letter.

As the date of Lady Titania's ball drew near, Celeste wrote His Grace another letter, this one pleading with him to allow her sisters to attend. *For I have done as you instructed and seen nothing of my family. If you would be so kind as to reward my obedience and grant me this one favor, I promise I shall ask for no more. The season is nearly at an end. Surely it could do no harm to bring forth my sisters now.*

The duke's reply thrilled her: *Do as you wish.*

An embossed invitation was sent off immediately.

There was much to be done to get ready for such a

The Wedding Deception 177

grand affair—flowers and refreshments to be ordered, invitations sent, new gowns fitted. *This is to be a wonderful ball,* Celeste wrote the duke. *I do wish you felt inclined to come.* She knew this was one wish His Grace wouldn't grant. But she would have loved to have him see her in all her finery. *As I wear the pearls you gave me I will think of you,* she concluded, and sealed the letter.

A week before the ball the ladies had a visitor. "Lord Greenfield!" exclaimed Celeste. "What a very pleasant surprise. Has the duke sent you to attend Lady Titania's ball in his place, or does he send you to tell me he has decided to come to London and attend it himself?

Lord Greenfield smiled, and Celeste noticed that it was not his usual broad grin. "Neither," he said. "I came to tell you the duke is unwell."

Celeste fell back onto her chair. "Unwell? How so?"

"He has contracted an inflammation of the lungs."

"The poor man," put in Lady Titania. "I hope he is taking plenty of broth."

"I must go to him," said Celeste.

"Don't be ridiculous, child," said Her Ladyship. "How silly to rush off simply because His Grace is indisposed."

"But he is sick," said Celeste.

"That does not put him at death's door," said Her Ladyship. "I should certainly find it disconcerting if every time I sneezed I had someone rushing to my bedside to measure me for my coffin."

"He is most unwell," said the earl.

"He will want me there," said Celeste firmly.

Lady Titania looked at Lord Greenfield. "Does the duke request Miss Hart return to him?"

"No, not precisely," began His Lordship.

"There," said Lady Titania, cutting him off. She turned to Celeste. "Did I not tell you as much? Now, my dear, you must at least stay until after the ball. It is only a week away. And who knows but that in a week the duke may be completely recovered?"

"Very well," said Celeste. "But if I do not hear he is recovered, I shall go to him the day after the ball."

Her Ladyship shrugged. "Suit yourself."

Lord Greenfield was shown out, and the look on his face left Celeste feeling anything but easy with her decision. He hadn't looked exactly disapproving, but he hadn't looked happy, either. Disappointed, perhaps? And if he was disappointed with her decision to remain, the duke must be feeling worse than Lord Greenfield had let on.

As the days went by she began to fret. Perhaps the duke was getting worse instead of better. Surely he would send a courier if he felt himself in grave danger. Perhaps he was too sick even to send someone. After all, he had sent someone, and she had turned him away.

Two days before the ball Celeste sent a message to Lord Greenfield and told Smythe to pack a trunk. "We leave for St. Feylands tomorrow," she informed her.

Smythe was startled into saying, "But the ball!"

"Will go on just fine without me," said Celeste.

Lady Titania was equally shocked with her guest's ill-timed departure. "Why, this ball is as much for you as anything," she protested.

"My family will be present to enjoy it. That will be enough for me," said Celeste. "And I certainly could find no pleasure in dancing knowing that the duke is ill."

The Wedding Deception   179

Lord Greenfield called and was ushered into the drawing room, where Celeste met him. "Can you escort me back to St. Feylands tomorrow?" she asked.

He smiled broadly. "It is what I have been waiting to do these past five days," he said. "We shall leave at first light."

"I hope he is not too very ill," said Celeste in a small voice.

"Just seeing you is bound to have its good effect," said the earl.

He took his leave and Lady Titania caught him at the door. "A word with you, Your Lordship," she said. "How bad is the duke, really?"

The earl looked at her soberly. "In truth, he is very ill. He forbade me to come right out and ask Celeste to attend him."

"Why?" demanded Her Ladyship. "What strange motive lies behind this?"

"You have known him these many years," replied the earl. "Can you not guess?"

Her Ladyship nodded. "I can, indeed," she said. "And I wonder why you go along with it."

"For honor's sake," said Greenfield.

"Bah! Anyone can see the child is worth twenty of any other of these milk-and-water misses without putting her to the test. I could have told him from the first day I met her that this girl was unlike Marie."

The earl's smile turned to stone.

"Oh, now, don't let your feathers get ruffled," said Her Ladyship. "Marie could not help how she was any more than St. Feylands could help being who he is. It was an unfortunate match. Nothing more." The earl still stood with his jaw set. "Well, never mind," she said. "I wish you well and Godspeed. And may I also be the first to wish you happy?" she added. teasingly.

The earl's face relaxed and he smiled. "I hope you may," he said.

15

Time crawled as Celeste and the earl made their way back to the castle. Every mile seemed an inch, every minute an hour. "How much longer?" Celeste asked as they waited for the horses to be changed.

"We are now in Gloucestershire. We shall be at the castle in time for dinner. And speaking of food, won't you take a glass of cider? It would do you good."

Celeste shook her head. "The thought of food makes me ill."

"You have eaten almost nothing the entire trip. You'll do the duke no good if you make yourself sick," said His Lordship.

"I shan't eat till I've seen him," she said.

The afternoon shadows had fallen by the time the tired horses pulled the earl's carriage up the drive to St. Feylands castle. Celeste jumped out as soon as the steps were let down, refusing to wait for the earl to hand her down. Mrs. Griffon had come out to meet her and she rushed to the housekeeper and took her hands. "How is he?"

Mrs. Griffon's lips were trembling. "He is very bad, Miss Hart."

Heedless of her coat and bonnet, Celeste ran up the stairway to the duke's room. Had the stairs always been this long and winding? Would she never reach the top? Oh, it was like a nightmare!

At last she gained the duke's room and pushed open the massive oak door. There he lay, in his huge Louis XVI bed. He looked so frail. So still. Like death. "Your Grace," cried Celeste, and ran to fall to her knees at the bedside. "I should never have left you," she sobbed. "Please get well. You must. I promise I will love you and never think of anyone else, and I'll never leave St. Feylands again. Only speak to me."

Thus delivered of her speech, Celeste buried her head in the covers and began to cry in earnest.

The duke raised a feeble hand and laid it on her head. "How is it you ask me to speak, then make such a noise you cannot hear me," he said in a weak voice. "And why are you wearing that ridiculous bonnet?"

Celeste raised a tearstained, smiling face to him. "You are alive."

"Yes," replied His Grace. "And I must say you took long enough to come see if I was."

"I was foolish. Lady Titania was sure you were not so very ill, and I let her talk me into remaining in London until after her ball."

The duke sighed and shut his eyes. "And how was the ball?" he asked.

"I don't know," said Celeste. "I left the day before."

The duke smiled. "Leave me now, child. I am tired."

"Yes, Your Grace," she said meekly.

The Wedding Deception

She passed the Earl of Greenfield on her way out. "I have given orders for an early dinner," he informed her. "I am sure you must be famished by now."

Celeste admitted she was, and left to change her clothes.

The duke did not open his eyes at Greenfield's approach. "You are not yet Duke of St. Feylands," he said.

"And you are in no shape to be ordering dinner," said the earl, unperturbed.

"Hmmph," said the duke, but a corner of his mouth turned up.

"You are tired," said the earl. "I shan't stay."

"Stay a moment," said His Grace. "That old sawbones thinks me ready for my grave, but I know different. Just seeing the girl has been a tonic." He opened his eyes and looked at the younger man. "So she didn't stay for the ball?"

Greenfield shook his head. "And she fretted all the way here." He smiled at the duke. "If I didn't know better, I'd swear you made yourself sick just for the pleasure of testing her character one last time."

His Grace smiled wearily and sighed. "No. But you must admit it was a good one. She is a fit bride."

"Good," began the earl.

"I know what you are thinking, Arthur," said His Lordship. "May I remind you of your promise to me?"

The earl frowned but said nothing.

"I would sleep," announced the duke.

"Sleep well," said Greenfield. He laid a comforting hand on the older man's arm and left him.

Greenfield stayed long enough to make sure the duke was out of danger, then took his leave, saying he had left his estate neglected too long. "If you like, I shall come visit you at your home during the Christmas holiday," he told Celeste as they stood at the castle door.

Surely there was nothing wrong in the earl coming to visit her family. "I should like that very much," said Celeste.

He smiled down at her. "So would I," he said.

She stood for a long time, watching his carriage drive off down the road, savoring the warm feeling inside her. She would have a wonderful Christmas, then come spring she would marry the duke and be the very best wife he ever had. She turned back inside the castle, telling herself it was only the cold wind that had made her shiver and stolen the smile from her face.

Although no longer sick, the duke did not quickly regain his strength. "You must eat more," Celeste chided him.

"Faugh. I have no appetite," he complained.

Celeste said nothing, but she worried, and although December was now upon them, she said nothing of going to her family.

In the middle of the month she received a letter from her mother. *If the duke is feeling strong enough, he is more than welcome to accompany you home for a Christmas visit. If not, I would hope he could spare you to us. You really should be returning home, anyway, dear child, as there is much to do if we are to have you ready for a wedding in May. What with your nuptials in May and Emily's in June, I fear I shall go distracted.*

Celeste smiled at this. She knew how her mother loved to plan entertainments, and with two weddings to plan she must be enjoying herself greatly. Celeste read on:

> *We were honored yesterday by a visit from the Earl of Greenfield, who had some sort of business with your father. Papa didn't tell me what it was about, which is very unlike him. He would only say that the earl came on a very pleasant business. Your father has invited him to dine with us tomorrow night, which is most agreeable with me. He is a nice young man and I think Dorothea cherishes certain hopes. Wouldn't it be delightful to have all three of my daughters happily married within the year!*

Celeste crumpled the paper. So the Earl of Greenfield had decided to court Dorothea. Well, and why shouldn't he? she asked herself reasonably. I cannot marry him.

She took out writing paper and penned a note to her mother, saying she couldn't yet leave the duke and wishing them all a merry Christmas.

Her Christmas with the duke was a quiet one. She had done her shopping in the village and sent presents off to all her family. For her future husband she had painted a portrait of him. It was a fanciful piece, picturing the duke in armor and seated on a white steed, with his castle in the background. She had painted a smile on his face, and made sure to put it in his eyes as well.

He inspected his present and chuckled.

"I put the smile back in your eyes," pointed out Celeste.

"That you have," said the duke, looking at her fondly. "Ah, I shall miss you," he said.

"Miss me?" Celeste was momentarily puzzled. "Oh," she said. "I suppose you mean I must soon return to my family."

"That, too," he said. "Here, now. No more stalling. You must open your present from me." He handed her a slim box wrapped in red ribbon.

She opened it and gasped. There on a bed of satin lay a diamond necklace such as Celeste had never seen. She looked at the duke, stunned.

"All the Duchesses of St. Feylands wear this necklace," said His Grace, "and I would wager that never before has it graced a neck more lovely or more deserving."

Celeste threw her arms around the duke and thanked him tearfully, all the while thinking that she had to be the least deserving female in all the world.

Shortly after Boxing day the Earl of Greenfield called at St. Feylands. "So," he said as the butler showed him into the drawing room, "I find you both holed up here instead of with the bride's family as any proper couple would be."

Celeste looked up, her face shining. "How good to see you, Your Lordship."

"Arthur," corrected the earl. "Remember?"

How could she help but remember? She said his name like a prayer every night before she went to bed. She blushed and lowered her gaze, watching as the earl kissed her hand.

"I looked for you in vain in Middlesex," he said.

Hope rose in her like a hot-air balloon. Was it just possible he hadn't gone to Middlesex to court Dorothea, but had gone looking for her as he'd promised? Naturally the duke, being unwell, would have corresponded little with the earl. How could he have known she was still at the castle? She wanted to jump up and hug Lord Greenfield's neck. Instead she calmly said, "We thought it best to stay here. What sense in risking the duke's health all for the sake of a cup of wassail drunk listening to my sisters' prattle?"

The corners of the earl's mouth twitched. "She becomes more like you every day," he told the duke.

Again, Celeste blushed. "Oh, dear," was all she could say.

But the duke smiled. "She has merely learned to be a practical woman who speaks her mind. Would that more females were like our Celeste."

"How did you find my family?" asked Celeste.

"Well, but missing you. Your father especially."

Celeste's smile turned wistful. This had been her first Christmas away from home, and although she'd tried not to think of it, she'd missed her father's merry laugh. "Next Christmas we'll be together," she said.

"I bring you Christmas greetings from everyone," continued the earl. "Oh, yes. And I have a present for you." He took out a small box and handed it to Celeste.

She tore at the wrapping, anxious to see what was inside. "Oh, my!" she exclaimed excitedly, and held up a heart-shaped locket. "How charming!"

"Do you like it, then?" asked the earl.

"I shall treasure it always," she said. Then, not wanting the duke to feel left out, she said, "How lucky can one lady be? I had a beautiful diamond necklace from His Grace which I am almost afraid to wear, it must be so valuable."

"I am afraid this one has little enough value, save what sentiment you may care to attach to it," said Greenfield.

"I shall attach much," said Celeste, and thought how much more valuable this simple locket was than the duke's grand necklace. "Well," she said, suddenly the efficient lady of the manor, "I think as we have company I had best instruct Cook to make some Christmas nog."

They had a grand dinner that night, and toasted each other with the cook's special Christmas punch. As they drank, an unbidden thought stole into Celeste's mind; Did the earl give Dorothea something for Christmas?

The earl didn't stay with them long enough for her to find out. Before the week was out he was gone, and Celeste and the duke fell once more into their old routine.

It seemed to Celeste that the duke was daily improving, and by the end of January he was once again his old self. And talking of sending her home.

She wasn't at all sure she wanted to go home to hear Dorothea prattling about the earl and her plans and schemes for snaring him. He loves me, thought Celeste. But he cannot marry me, she concluded sadly, and it is hardly fair to expect him to wear the willow for me.

In February her mother wrote urging her to come home to begin fittings for her bridal gown, and at the end of the month the earl sent her off in his carriage.

Her family was happy to welcome her back. "My little girl has turned into a grown woman," said her father fondly. "Life with the duke agrees with you."

"You do look wonderful," agreed Emily.

Even Dorothea had a kind word for her on her first evening home. "You will make a lovely duchess," she said as they sat in the drawing room, awaiting the summons to dinner. Dorothea sighed happily. "Just think what life would have been like if you hadn't gone to stay with the duke! We'd never have met the Earl of Greenfield."

Celeste felt herself go rigid. What happened between Greenfield and Dorothea when he made his visit to her family? Perhaps more than the earl had told her. After all, he owed her no explanations. He was free to court whomever he pleased.

"I wish I weren't engaged to Edward," Emily was saying.

"Oh, Em. Do stop complaining," said Dorothea. "It is all you have done since you accepted him."

"And so should you complain if you were in my slippers," said Emily. "Edward is not half so exciting as the Earl of Greenfield."

"You would never have caught Greenfield, anyway," said Dorothea with a superior smile.

"You may not catch him yourself," said Emily. "You really should have made a push to interest that fine duke you met at Lady Titania's ball."

"I prefer Lord Greenfield," said Dorothea.

"I don't see him making a push to secure your hand," observed Emily.

"Why on earth do you think he called on us at Christmas?" retorted Dorothea. "And once Celeste marries the duke, our families will be so closely linked we shall be seeing much of each other. I wager we'll be engaged by next Christmas."

The butler announced dinner. Celeste rose and went with her family to the dining room, but she no longer had any appetite.

16

Mr. and Mrs. Hart planned a ball to celebrate the upcoming nuptials of their daughters. It was to be a grand affair, held the week before Celeste's wedding. Invitations had been sent to their neighbors along the Thames as well as some of the new friends they had made in London during the Little Season.

Edward Finch was very nervous about the upcoming affair and confessed to Emily that he wasn't at all sure he liked having to hobnob with such a grand personage as a duke.

"You merely have to greet him," said Emily patiently. "Then you may avoid him the rest of the evening. I assure you, it is what I intend to do, for he makes me nervous as a goose at Christmas. How Celeste ever bore spending so much time with him I cannot imagine, and I certainly don't envy her, even if she will be a duchess."

Nor did Dorothea, for she had set her cap for a certain handsome earl. Anticipation of success gave her a generosity of heart toward her little sister, and she was even so kind as to tell Celeste the day before the ball how pretty she would look in her pink flounced ball gown.

"But not half so pretty as she will look next week in her wedding gown," said her mama fondly. "Such fine lace I found for it in London. And how fortunate we are to have such an excellent dressmaker within five miles of our home!"

Celeste tried to look happy, but her smiles had been growing weaker with every passing month, and the small movement of her lips barely passed for a smile.

"Such a tiny smile, my dear," coaxed her mother. "Surely you can do better than that. For a bride-to-be about to have a wonderful ball in her honor you don't look at all happy."

"I'm sorry, Mama," said Celeste.

Her mother looked at the small amount of food her daughter had been pushing around her plate and asked, "Are you not felling well, dearest?"

"I'm just a little tired," said Celeste. "I shall be fine."

"Not if you don't force yourself to eat more," said her mother, and it made Celeste remember her words to the duke only a few months before.

She sighed. "Perhaps I will let Dorothea and Em go into the village without me. I really have no need of anything, and I am rather tired."

"An outing might make you feel better," suggested her mother.

Celeste merely shook her head.

"At least eat a little of your breakfast," pleaded Mrs. Hart. "If you don't eat more, your wedding dress will hang on you."

The mention of her wedding took away what little appetite Celeste had left.

That afternoon while her sisters went into the village to shop for ribbon and fans for the ball, Celeste sat on the lawn overlooking the Thames and dreamed and sketched. Before she knew it, she had filled several sheets with portraits of the Earl of Greenfield.

"If only I were an artist!" said a voice behind her.

She gave a start and turned to see the earl. Blushing, she hurriedly put her papers together. "Your Lordship! I did not expect to see you here," she said, still too embarrassed to raise her face to look at him.

"Not be here for your ball?" he chided. "You must think me a poor friend, indeed."

"Oh, never," said Celeste fervently.

The earl smiled. "Will you save me a waltz?" he asked.

She nodded.

"What were you drawing?" he asked. "Not more pictures of your sisters as donkeys?"

She blushed afresh. "No. It is nothing." She snatched up the papers and hugged them to her.

"Are they of me?" he asked.

"I must go in now," she said, and ran toward the house.

The earl tried to follow her, but Dorothea and Emily were home again and had come in search of him, and with a sister on each side he remained on the lawn.

But he found her the following night at the ball, sitting next to the duke, who had arrived that very afternoon. "I suppose you have come to steal Celeste away for a dance," said the duke.

"That is the purpose of balls," replied Lord Greenfield gaily. "And as you detest dancing, I am sure you won't mind me relieving you of your painful duty."

The duke waved them away. "Be gone," he said.

"This is the last time I shall dance with you before your wedding," said the earl as they glided across the ballroom floor.

"You will dance with me on my wedding day, won't you?" asked Celeste.

"Every dance, if you wish," he replied.

If this answer had been meant to make her happy, it didn't succeed. She bit her trembling lip and blinked hard to push back the tears.

"Celeste, you do love me, don't you?" he asked softly.

"Oh, please. Let's just enjoy this moment," she begged.

"I know you love me, but I must hear it from your lips. I must know before your wedding day," he insisted.

She looked at him and her face told all. "You know I do," she said in anguished tones. "Now you must never ask me again."

"I shan't have to," he said, and twirled them in a dizzying circle.

A Faerie-tale Wedding

Celeste stood before her looking glass and stared at the sad-eyed creature in white satin looking back at her. "You look so lovely, miss," said Smythe. "Just like a fairy-tale princess."

Celeste sighed. "I wish," she began, then bit her lip. It would hardly be proper to say what she was thinking, that she wished a handsome prince would come and rescue her. How ungrateful! It was not as if she were marrying an ogre. She was marrying her dear duke, who needed her so. She would be happy. She would! Her eyes began to sting and she blinked hard.

"Such a lovely sight!" exclaimed her mother, walking into her room. "And it is such a lovely day. Happy the bride the sun shines on, they say."

Celeste nodded dumbly.

"The carriage is waiting," said Mrs. Hart. She put an arm around her daughter's shoulders and gave her an encouraging hug as she led her to the door. "Such a lovely wedding breakfast we have planned. And I know the duke will be all that is considerate tonight."

At this Celeste's step faltered, but her mother led her on, assuring her all would be well, predicting a happy future.

The guests were seated and waiting inside the church when the bride and her mother and sisters arrived, and the duke was waiting in the vestibule, Mr. Hart bearing him company. "Oh, Your Grace!" cried Mrs. Hart. "'Tis bad luck for the groom to see the bride before the wedding ceremony."

"And well I know it," said the duke cheerfully. "Which is why my son is waiting in the sanctuary."

Mrs. Hart stared at the duke as if he had lost his mind and her husband laughed merrily. "You must forgive me for not telling you, my dear," said her husband. "I was afraid you might not be inclined to keep a secret."

"A secret!" exclaimed his wife, pardonably angered. "You talk as though we were speaking of a birthday present and not my daughter's wedding." She turned her anger on the duke. "And who, pray, is your son?"

The duke smiled. "A man who loves your daughter very much." He turned to Celeste. "You must forgive me for misleading you so. I made my son promise to go along with my scheme. You see, word of Mr. Hart's amazingly beautiful and sweet child had reached him last season, and he was already more than a little in love with you. But I, being a bitter old man, did not believe such a paragon existed outside a storybook.

"When your father wrote to me of his misfortunes, I devised a plan to meet you and see for myself if you were worthy of such a fine man as my son. I tested you in every way, and never did you fail. You were always unselfish, both in your concern for your family and in your loyalty to myself. My first wife never would have left the pleasures of London for a place beside a sickbed, I can assure you."

At this Celeste, who had been standing mutely in shock, burst into tears. "Oh, Your Grace, I don't deserve such praise, for I loved another. And I cannot marry your son."

The duke looked shocked. "Not marry the Earl of Greenfield?"

Now it was Celeste's turn to look shocked. The duke chuckled. Dorothea, who had been standing behind her sister, moaned and fainted, and Celeste gripped her mother's arm. "But I don't understand," she said. "I thought I was to become the Duchess St. Feylands."

"And so you will be one day, when Arthur comes into the title."

"It was all a trick?" Celeste was talking to herself as much as anyone.

The duke took her hand. "You must forgive me, child. Arthur is a good man. He deserved better in a wife than I received, which is why I bullied him into silence."

"If you don't wish to marry the earl, you have only to say so, dearest," said her mother.

"Oh, Mama. It is what I have wished for the longest time," cried Celeste happily, and she hugged the duke. "Dearest, kindest of men! How can I thank you?"

"By being the kind and loving daughter you have been to me from the start," said His Grace. "Now, perhaps your mother and I had best take our seats so your father can escort you down the aisle."

* * *

All who attended the wedding of Miss Celeste Hart to the Earl of Greenfield, future Duke of St. Feylands, agreed that never before had they seen a more beautiful bride or a more handsome bridegroom. Nor had they heard wedding vows more poignantly exchanged. The maid of honor looked a little wan, but it was to be expected. The poor eldest Miss Hart had been the hardest hit by her father's misfortunes. A few whispered they thought it very unfair that the youngest daughter (who was barely even out, for goodness' sake) should be married first.

But those who knew the family well agreed that fate had played fair with the Hart daughters, and when the bride and groom kissed, all present sighed happily, sure that the couple would live happily ever after.

FROM THE ACCLAIMED AUTHOR OF
SEA OF DREAMS

TOUCH OF LACE
Elizabeth DeLancey

*They shared a promise to cherish forever—
and a journey of dreams and desire...*

Anna left Ireland for the promise of America. Stephen vowed to build a new life for his young son. Their voyage west bound them to a bold deception, for Anna had to defend herself from a perilous destiny with a hasty marriage to Stephen. But their vow to love and honor was only the beginning of a tempestuous passion...

Praise for Sea of Dreams:
"A moving love story with the perfect mix
of tenderness and adventure!"
—Jill Marie Landis, bestselling author of *Come Spring*

__1-55773-851-3/$4.99 (On sale June 1993)

For Visa, MasterCard and American Express ($15 minimum) orders call: 1-800-631-8571

FOR MAIL ORDERS: CHECK BOOK(S). FILL OUT COUPON. SEND TO: BERKLEY PUBLISHING GROUP 390 Murray Hill Pkwy., Dept. B East Rutherford, NJ 07073 NAME———————————— ADDRESS————————— CITY——————————— STATE ——————— ZIP——— PLEASE ALLOW 6 WEEKS FOR DELIVERY. PRICES ARE SUBJECT TO CHANGE WITHOUT NOTICE.	POSTAGE AND HANDLING: $1.75 for one book, 75¢ for each additional. Do not exceed $5.50. BOOK TOTAL $ ____ POSTAGE & HANDLING $ ____ APPLICABLE SALES TAX $ ____ (CA, NJ, NY, PA) TOTAL AMOUNT DUE $ ____ PAYABLE IN US FUNDS. (No cash orders accepted.)

Nationally bestselling author
JILL MARIE LANDIS

___COME SPRING 0-515-10861-8/$4.99
"This is a world-class novel ... it's fabulous!"
—Bestselling author Linda Lael Miller
She canceled her wedding, longing to explore the wide open West. But nothing could prepare her Bostonian gentility for an adventure that thrust her into the arms of a wild mountain man....

___JADE 0-515-10591-0/$4.95
A determined young woman of exotic beauty returned to San Francisco to unveil the secrets behind her father's death. But her bold venture would lead her to recover a family fortune-and discover a perilous love.

___ROSE 0-515-10346-2/$4.50
"A gentle romance that will warm your soul."—Heartland Critiques
When Rosa set out from Italy to join her husband in Wyoming, little did she know that fate held heartbreak ahead. Suddenly a woman alone, the challenge seemed as vast as the prairies.

___SUNFLOWER 0-515-10659-3/$4.99
"A winning novel!"—Publishers Weekly
Analisa was strong and independent. Caleb had a brutal heritage that challenged every feeling in her heart. Yet their love was as inevitable as the sunrise....

___WILDFLOWER 0-515-10102-8/$4.95
"A delight from start to finish!"—Rendezvous
From the great peaks of the West to the lush seclusion of a Caribbean jungle, Dani and Troy discovered the deepest treasures of the heart.

For Visa, MasterCard and American Express orders ($15 minimum) call: 1-800-631-8571

FOR MAIL ORDERS: CHECK BOOK(S).
FILL OUT COUPON. SEND TO:

BERKLEY PUBLISHING GROUP
390 Murray Hill Pkwy., Dept. B
East Rutherford, NJ 07073

NAME_____
ADDRESS_____
CITY_____
STATE_____ZIP_____

PLEASE ALLOW 6 WEEKS FOR DELIVERY.
PRICES ARE SUBJECT TO CHANGE WITHOUT NOTICE.

POSTAGE AND HANDLING:
$1.75 for one book, 75¢ for each additional. Do not exceed $5.50.

BOOK TOTAL $_____
POSTAGE & HANDLING $_____
APPLICABLE SALES TAX $_____
(CA, NJ, NY, PA)
TOTAL AMOUNT DUE $_____

PAYABLE IN US FUNDS.
(No cash orders accepted.)

Eavesdropping on Love . . .

Curiosity made Celeste's steps slow. The sound of voices drifted out to her and she drew near the door.

There was a long silence. "I have fallen in love with the girl," said the earl.

"Bah," spat the duke. "In two days' time? Don't be ridiculous."

"I am not being ridiculous," replied the earl. "You know I have seen enough young ladies to know a rare one when I see her, and may I remind you that I am certainly old enough—"

"You are old enough to do a great many things," interrupted the duke. "But you are not yet in my shoes!"

The duke's voice was rising. Even as Celeste backed away the duke's angry words followed her. "I am still head of this household and I forbid you—" She stopped her ears and ran off down the hall, tears running from her eyes. . . .

Diamond Books by Sheila Rabe

FAINT HEART
THE IMPROPER MISS PRYM
THE LOST HEIR
LADY LUCK
THE WEDDING DECEPTION